BLOWN AWAY!

The cloaked form dashed directly at the carriage, swooped close behind the footman and tossed something over the red-coated man's shoulders and into the carriage.

Longarm felt a sickness in his belly and leaped forward.

He was much too late, though.

And whoever cut the fuse on the bomb knew his business all too well. There was no time for anyone inside the carriage to react.

A flash of orange and red flame filled the windows of the rig, and a sharp, loud report boomed out to fill Colfax and stun the crowd into immobility.

TABOR EVANS

LONGARM

AND THE RENEGADE ASSASSINS

J

JOVE BOOKS, NEW YORK

LONGARM AND THE RENEGADE ASSASSINS

A Jove Book / published by arrangement with
the author

PRINTING HISTORY
Jove edition / June 1998

All rights reserved.
Copyright © 1998 by Jove Publications, Inc.
This book may not be reproduced in whole
or in part, by mimeograph or any other means,
without permission. For information address:
The Berkley Publishing Group, a member of Penguin Putnam Inc.,
200 Madison Avenue, New York, New York 10016.

The Penguin Putnam Inc. World Wide Web site address is
http://www.penguinputnam.com

ISBN: 0-515-12292-0

A JOVE BOOK®
Jove Books are published by The Berkley Publishing Group,
a member of Penguin Putnam Inc.,
200 Madison Avenue, New York, New York 10016.
JOVE and the "J" design are trademarks
belonging to Jove Publications, Inc.

PRINTED IN THE UNITED STATES OF AMERICA

10 9 8 7 6 5 4 3 2 1

LONGARM

AND THE
RENEGADE ASSASSINS

Chapter 1

United States Marshal William Vail, chief marshal of the Justice Department's Denver, Colorado, office, leaned back in his creaking, spring-loaded swivel chair and closely scrutinized the piece of paper his top deputy had just handed him.

"Look, uh, I know this is kinda sudden, Billy," U.S. Deputy Marshal Custis Long tried to explain, "but . . ."

"Shhh, I'm concentrating."

"Yes, sir. Sorry." Which he wasn't, but it sounded nice and polite. And politeness counts for a lot when one is seeking favors.

The deputy known usually, at least to his friends and closest enemies, as Longarm stood up, impatient, and began to pace Billy Vail's office while he waited for his boss to finish reading.

Longarm was a tall man, something over six feet in height, with a horseman's lean build, broad shoulders, and a craggy, sun- and wind-burned face. He had brown hair, brown eyes, and a large handlebar mustache. He wore a Colt revolver strapped at his waist in a cross-draw rig carried just to the left of his belt buckle, and a derringer carried much less conspicuously in his vest pocket where an ordinary watch fob would have been expected. Normally calm and unexcitable, this morning Longarm was more than a little nervous.

Billy Vail glanced up at him and observed, "The lady must be something special."

"Lady? That request doesn't say anything about any ladies."

The marshal smiled. "How long have I known you, Longarm? Ten years or more? I think by now I know what's up when you come rushing in here at the last moment and ask to take actual leave time starting immediately. Not just a couple days off, mind. But time charged against your annual leave? Custis, you surprise me with this. And you haven't surprised me in an awfully long time now."

Longarm didn't bother arguing with his boss. There would have been no point. Once Billy decided on a point of view, it would take some serious proofs to the contrary if one expected to make the man change his mind.

Besides, Billy was right. There *was* a lady involved in Longarm's desire to take an unannounced holiday in the mountains west of Denver. A very special lady indeed. And if he let this one get away, well . . .

"Well?" Longarm asked, unable to contain the question any longer.

Vail smiled. "Sure, you can have the time off. The rest of this week and . . . what was it you wanted? Until next Thursday too. Will that suit you?"

"Perfect," Longarm enthused. "Just what the doctor ordered." Or if not the doctor, then the nurse, although he kept that to himself. "Thanks."

"One thing," Billy cautioned.

"What's that?"

"Before you go, Longarm, I want you to help me show the colors here at noon."

"Show the colors? I don't understand. You want me to do something with the flag, Boss?"

"I didn't mean literally. But I want a nice show of

2

force from as many of our people as we can put together this morning. There is a very important visitor I want you all seen by.''

''Mm?''

''A close friend of the president, actually. He's been appointed Special Commissioner for Indian Affairs and sent here to look into the question of grazing rights on the Ute lands.''

Longarm grimaced. He was familiar with that particularly thorny problem. There was a large and highly vocal contingent of stockmen, ranchers who raised both beef and sheep, who felt they should have the right to graze unfenced lands including those claimed by the Ute nation. And there was a smaller but equally vocal group of moralizers, most of them not Coloradans at all, but fainthearted folks from back East who Longarm privately referred to as the Lo! the Poor Indian crowd, who supported Ute demands that the open lands be kept free of privately held livestock and available only to the Indians for their own hunting needs.

Neither side had yet expressed any willingness to compromise.

And each had solid political influence, the ranchers receiving support from senators and congressmen representing voting blocs in the West, and the Indians' supporters enjoying the support of politicians in the East, and Midwest. Southern politicians seemed indifferent to the question; they had their own problems.

In any event, Longarm knew the question was a potentially explosive one, and whoever won this small and seemingly insignificant battle might well achieve a superiority of power that would carry over into other decisions for months or years to come, certainly until the next congressional elections, and possibly much longer. So yes, this visitor was important indeed, and could well have much influence on the entire western part of the country.

"The U.S. attorney and I will be hosting a luncheon for the commissioner and his wife," Billy explained. "At the Cargile Club," he added.

Longarm's eyebrows went up and he whistled. "Fancy," he said. Which was something of an understatement. The Cargile was without question the grandest, most elegant—and most expensive—outfit ever to hit Denver. Or probably anyplace else between San Francisco and—Longarm didn't know, maybe Boston. Anyway, it was one highfalutin son of a bitch.

"I could wait until afternoon," Longarm offered, "if you'd take me with you." After all, going as the guest of someone with money and influence was the only way Custis Long would ever be allowed through the gilded doors of a place as tony as the Cargile Club.

"You know I'd take you except that you're officially off duty now."

"You haven't signed that leave request yet," Longarm pointed out.

"No? I thought I had." Billy examined the form in his hand, leaned forward, and plucked his pen from the inkwell. He scrawled a signature onto the paper and said, "Of course I did. See there?"

Longarm chuckled and went gratefully out to the main office to wait for the informal reception to welcome the visiting dignitary. After all, he had his days off. That was what counted here.

"Good-bye, sir. Good-bye, all."

Longarm stood among those who had drifted outside to see the party off to their luncheon. Longarm didn't have any idea what the ass-kissers expected to accomplish by clinging to the coattails of the commissioner and his lady. Longarm's motive in going along was to get the hell out of the building so he could grab a hackney and head for the hospital to tell Deborah that he would pick her up at the end of her shift. And after

4

that . . . He grinned, thinking about what would come after that.

A carriage had been arranged for the short journey from the Federal Building on Colfax Avenue up past the State Capitol and on to the Cargile Club. The carriage was a handsome thing drawn by a sleek and perfectly matched four-up of dappled grays. Damned horses even had purple plumes on their headstalls. Which seemed a bit much in Longarm's opinion, but then what in hell did he know about how a body is supposed to act when he's rich and important. That was unexplored territory as far as Deputy Long was concerned.

"Bye," Longarm mumbled softly as those around him called out best wishes. "Bet you ain't gonna have near as much fun as me," he added half under his breath so no one else could hear.

The commissioner and his wife were helped into the carriage by a fellow in some sort of red coat. Then the U.S. attorney and Billy Vail climbed in with somewhat less pomp and circumstance. The man in the red coat bent down to fold the steel steps away.

As he did so, a figure broke from the crowd that had gathered to see what all the carrying-on was about. The person was slight of frame and was wrapped in a heavy cloak. Longarm had a brief impression of long, black hair, tall boots beneath the hem of the swirling cloak . . . and a stream of thin smoke trailing from the running figure's hand.

The cloaked form dashed directly at the carriage, swooped close behind the footman, and tossed something over the red-coated man's shoulders and into the carriage.

Longarm felt a sickness in his belly and leaped forward.

He was much too late, though.

And whoever had cut the fuse on the bomb knew his

business all too well. There was no time for anyone inside the carriage to react.

A flash of orange and red flame filled the windows of the rig, and a sharp, loud report boomed out to fill Colfax and stun the crowd into immobility.

The body of the carriage seemed to bulge, then to sag as the frame was broken and the body ripped apart. The back end broke completely away from the front part of the rig, and the terrified team dragged what was left of the wreckage down the street at as hard a run as they could manage.

Lying on the cobblestones where the entire carriage had been was the back end of the broken vehicle surrounded by bits of lacquered and charred wood.

And a broken body wearing a gay dress covered with ruffles and with blood.

Longarm tried to push his way through a suddenly hysterical crowd, his Colt held high as he hoped for a shot at the bomber.

But the bomber was gone. Vanished as completely as the smoke that had trailed from the fuse of the cowardly bastard's bomb.

Longarm ran across to the other side of the street, then back again to move through the now-noisy crowd of onlookers.

There was no sign of the person in the cloak.

The only thing left behind was the stink of exploded powder.

And the destruction wrought by the bomb.

Jesus! Longarm thought suddenly. Billy. Billy Vail had been inside that carriage too.

Longarm whirled and ran as hard as he could down Colfax in the direction the shattered carriage had been dragged.

Chapter 2

Longarm did not own a black suit, but for this occasion he'd gone out and rented one. There was not another person in the whole miserable, stinking world he would have done that for. Anyone else, well, a black armband would be enough to show respect. But for Billy Vail . . .

The funeral, actually, was for all four victims of the bombing. But Billy was the only one of the four that Longarm cared about.

No, that was not right. Not really. He cared that the commissioner and his wife and the U.S. attorney were dead. No one deserved a death like that. But it was Billy that Longarm grieved for.

Billy Vail wasn't just a good boss. He was—had been—a good man. And there aren't so many of those around that the world can afford to lose them. Or throw them away, which seemed more the case here.

Longarm seethed with a desire to find the sons of bitches who'd planned this attack. First thing, he swore. If he had to turn in his badge and go after them on his own, he *would*, by damn, find them.

And when he did, he hoped to hell they tried to resist, because it would be a true joy to blow the fuckers away. Each and every one of them.

Just as soon as the funeral service was ended, Longarm figured to get started on his quest. He would—

"Psst!"

Longarm glanced to his right. Billy's clerk Henry was there, pale and drawn. Henry looked like he hadn't slept in the two days since the explosion, and behind the blank glare that reflected off his spectacles, Longarm thought he could see moisture welling up in Henry's eyes. Not that Longarm could blame him. Longarm felt like that himself; it was about all he could do to keep from giving in to an impulse that he hadn't felt since he took to wearing long pants.

"What is it, Henry?"

"Did they find you to tell you about the meeting?"

"I haven't talked to anybody from the office since . . . since it happened. What meeting?"

"It's in the U.S. attorney's office, Longarm. Right after the ceremony here."

"I don't care about . . ."

"If you want to help find who did this, you'll care and you'll damned well be there." That was strong language for the normally mild Henry.

"You know I want that more'n anything else in this world, Henry," Longarm told him.

"Then you'd best show up and see what each of us can do to bring these bastards in."

Longarm paused. Then nodded. "I'll be there."

Out in front of the throng of politicians, sycophants, and genuine friends, a preacher, a man Longarm had never seen before, was droning to the conclusion of an overlong eulogy that praised to the skies the recently deceased commissioner from Washington City, but that barely mentioned either Billy or the Denver-based U.S. attorney.

Not that any of that mattered, the way Longarm saw it. If there was a God—right now Longarm wasn't so damn certain about that—but if there was one, well, then

8

he already knew the sort of man Billy'd been and would throw open the Pearly Gates to welcome so fine a newcomer. And if there wasn't, then it didn't matter anyhow.

For Billy's sake, though, Longarm found himself hoping there was someone on the other side to give that good man a handshake and a big welcome when he walked out onto his cloud and signed for his new harp.

Longarm was so wrapped up in thinking about things like that that he was taken by surprise when the preacher all of a sudden wound up the proceedings and stepped back so the mourners could file past the four brightly polished coffins, each draped with a U.S. flag and covered in bright flowers.

Longarm and Henry joined the line of people passing by the coffins. It bothered Longarm that he didn't even know which one of them held Billy's mortal remains. They weren't any of them marked that Longarm could see, although presumably the undertaker knew which box was to go where.

Eventually all the public tears were shed and the final words had been spoken. A large hearse took two of the coffins away and headed in the direction of the railroad depot. Those, then, would be the bodies of the commissioner and his wife.

The other two, each in a smaller and less ornate hearse, were carried off toward the respective cemeteries chosen by the widows of the dead Denver men.

Longarm, still with Henry beside him, paid his respects to Mrs. Vail. He was going to have to remember, he reminded himself, to call on her every now and then and see what he might do to help ease her burden. God, he hoped Billy had left her well provided for, because the government would only give her a pittance for a pension, if it bothered to give her anything at all. Then, his heart near to breaking, he turned away.

He decided against going on to the cemetery to see

Billy's coffin put underground. This right here had been bad enough.

Besides, dammit, there was a pursuit to organize, and the sooner that was done the better.

"Come along, Custis. I have a hackney waiting around the corner."

Longarm nodded and, without protest, allowed Henry to lead him away from the saddest and most miserable damn thing he'd ever in his life had to do.

God, this was bad.

Chapter 3

Longarm leaned forward to flick the butt of a cheroot out of the cab window, then slouched back onto the worn padding of the seat. He felt lousy. But then this was one truly lousy day in every way that counted.

"Long. Custis."

"Yes, Henry?"

"Could I . . . could I ask you something."

"Yeah, of course." Longarm continued to peer out the window, not really focusing on anything, his expression vacant and miserable.

"The . . . I remember the other day seeing you run after the carriage, what was left of it."

"Uh-huh."

"And today . . . those coffins being closed."

"Yes?"

"Was it bad?"

The scene came all too readily back into Longarm's memory. Just like it had been that day.

"It was bad," he said softly, not wanting to go over it again in his mind, but knowing Henry was entitled to an answer. Henry had cared for Billy every bit as much as Longarm did. No, that probably wasn't true either. Henry very probably cared for Billy Vail even more than

Longarm. They'd worked together every day, and were much more than boss and employee. They'd been friends. That was one of Billy Vail's many gifts. He was able to command more than mere loyalty from the people he worked with. He was able to generate love as well.

"Time I caught up with them," Longarm went on, "there was already an ambulance there. I don't know how they got there so quick, but they did, and I know they were trying their best. The carriage was torn all to pieces. The whole back end of it was laying in the street back by the Federal Building. That and Mrs. Troutman's body.

"The ambulance attendants were picking up the commissioner when I got there. They had the back end of the ambulance open, and they were putting the commissioner on a stretcher. I could see that part of his leg"— Longarm paused, frowning in thought—"his right leg, I think it was, was missing. I remember that real clear because one of the men on the ambulance after they put the stretcher inside, he reached down and picked up the missing piece of leg and laid it onto the stretcher beside where it should've gone if it hadn't got blowed off."

"Jesus, God," Henry said, whispering it in such a way that Longarm didn't take it for blasphemy but for a sort of prayer instead.

"Billy and Mr. Terrell..." Longarm squeezed his eyes shut for a moment, although he kept his face turned away so Henry wouldn't see. "I tell you true, Henry, I never seen so much blood. They was both covered with it from top to toe. It was . . . it was pretty awful."

"The thing is . . . d'you think he suffered?" Henry asked. "That's what I've been worrying over ever since it happened. Did he suffer any?"

"That much blood . . . I don't expect he would have. He must have died quick, I think."

"He wasn't moving when they picked him up?"

"No, nor the attorney. The only one that showed any life was the commissioner, and he was screaming and losing blood in great, awful gouts of the stuff. I doubt he lasted halfway to the hospital unless they managed to get the bleeding stopped somehow."

"But the marshal . . . ?"

"I never saw him move at all. He just laid there all awash in blood, and they picked him up and then Terrell, and after that they were clanging the bell and running like hell toward the hospital."

"You didn't follow after them?"

"Not then. I circled back and walked the streets some, thinking I could maybe spot the bomber trying to slip away unnoticed. But I never saw anything more of him. I expect he got rid of the cloak right away, and I don't know about you but I never saw what he had on under it, so I prob'ly could've walked right past him on the sidewalk and never known it. Later on that evening I went over to the hospital. They told me none of them made it. I can't say I was surprised. But you gotta hope. You know?"

"I know. I was there too that afternoon. It wasn't news I wanted to get," Henry said.

"We're gonna find whoever threw that bomb, Henry. I swear we are."

"I hope I'm there when it happens," Henry said in a coldly bitter tone. Longarm looked at him. Henry might look meek and bookish. And for the most part he genuinely was. But the little man had more grit than enough, and Longarm knew he could turn loose with a six-gun when he had to. No doubt that was what Henry had in mind now, a chance to put some lead into whatever son of a mangy bitch it was who'd murdered Billy Vail.

Longarm stared back out the window, his eyes red and stinging for some reason.

God, this was bad.

Chapter 4

The U.S. attorney's office was bigger than Billy Vail's had been, but even so, it could hardly hold everybody. Longarm felt like a sardine in a can, an overly warm can at that, wedged in as he was between Henry and Smiley so that his arms were about pinned to his sides. If he'd farted, the guy behind him would have felt the breeze. In addition to every deputy working out of the Denver office, there was a contingent of U.S. deputy marshals who had been rushed in on loan from Kansas City and four more from San Francisco. There were representatives from the law-enforcing bodies of the state of Colorado, the cities of Denver, Aurora, Golden, and Central City, and Denver and Arapaho Counties. Hell, Longarm didn't know where-all else these people came from. There was even a pair of Secret Service agents—cold-eyed men who looked like they suspected everyone there but themselves—who'd been dispatched off the president's own protection detail and sent to keep an eye on the investigation.

The one thing all of these people seemed to have in common, Longarm thought, was that every swinging dick among them wanted to catch the bastards who'd killed Billy Vail and Avery Terrell and George and Mrs.

Troutman. From every jurisdiction around, and with whatever motivations there were that drove them, these boys all looked just about as offended and anxious to get on with it as Longarm was himself.

"All right, settle down now. Everybody listen up," a voice called from the front of room, from what had been U.S. Attorney Terrell's desk. The room, which a moment earlier had been softly buzzing with the combined noise of several dozen simultaneous conversations, became instantly silent.

"Thank you," the voice went on.

Longarm tried to get a look at whoever was doing the talking, but all he could see at the moment was the top of the man's head. Which did not exactly give him much to go on.

"For those of you who do not know me," the speaker announced, "my name is Cotton. J. B. Cotton. I am—I should say that I was—assistant U.S. attorney under Avery Terrell. The Attorney General of the United States has appointed me interim U.S. attorney for this district until such time as permanent replacements can be decided upon to fill this vacancy and that of the U.S. marshal for the district." He paused and coughed. "It is my understanding that no decision has been made yet about whether another special envoy will be named to fill the shoes of Commissioner Troutman. All of those decisions, naturally, will be at the will of the president and Congress. In the meantime, gentlemen, it is our task— one might even say it will be our privilege—to conduct a swift and sure investigation into the shocking and unwarranted assault on our brothers in service of our government. It is up to us, each one of us assembled here today, to see that the murderers do not go unpunished, to insure that the lives of these brave and worthy men were not given up in vain.

"I am, on the authority of the President of these United States, assuming command of the investigation.

15

I will assign tasks to each of you, and I will expect you, individually and collectively, to carry out this work with all the diligence and expertise that is available to you. I expect you to give this your total attention. A few of you, quite naturally, will be required to perform the ordinary duties of your respective jurisdictions and agencies. When you are given such tasks, I expect your full cooperation. This investigation is too important to allow the intrusion of personalities or politics into any of the decisions. Those of you who must perform other duties should do so with the understanding that your cooperation and your devotion to matters that may at the time seem insignificant are necessary so that others can labor on a full-time basis toward the discovery and apprehension of whoever it was who planned the recent attack on the commissioner and his wife.

"I want you to know that I personally will not rest until these people, every one of them who may have been involved, have been caught, convicted, and sentenced to the fullest extent of the law. I trust that everyone else in this room feels the same. If you do not, please have the courtesy to speak up now. I want no shirkers on this team, gentlemen. I expect every man among you to commit himself to his best efforts, without regard to personalities or favoritism. Is there anyone here who is not willing to make this commitment? Anyone at all? Speak now, please, if you want out."

Longarm would have been damned well amazed if anyone had asked out. And, of course, no one did—as the interim U.S. attorney undoubtedly had expected. These men wouldn't have come if they and their bosses hadn't been personally and completely pissed off by the cowardly bomb attack. Those of them that still had bosses, that is.

Which, dammit, left out Longarm and Henry and all the other deputies who'd worked under Billy Vail's leadership. It looked like for the time being they didn't have a boss and weren't fixing to get a new one.

Still, that was all right. The new broom, whoever he turned out to be, might well want to sweep the office clean of old associations and old loyalties. The next U.S. marshal could turn out to be a politician who would want his own people on the payroll. And Custis Long couldn't have borne the thought right now of not being a part of the investigation into Billy's death. He could live with the idea of being fired so some political ass-kisser could replace him. Hell, he'd been fired from jobs before. But he couldn't—wouldn't—accept it until or unless the person or persons responsible for that bombing were behind bars or, better yet, dead and cooling in the hard, heartless ground.

"Give me your best efforts," Cotton was saying, "and we will all work together to find these people and bring them to justice. Give me your best efforts, and together we will accomplish that worthy task. Give me your best efforts, each and every one, I beg you." Cotton paused again. "Now, if you will please be patient with me, I have made up a list of assignments for those I knew would be here. I will read the names off and tell you which room to report to to be briefed on what will be expected of you. Anyone left when I have completed the list—that is to say, those from neighboring jurisdictions who I may not have anticipated seeing today—will please wait in this room until the others have left. Then I will ask you to register your name, affiliation, and areas of expertise with my clerk Ralph Hodges. Is that clear? Fine. First, then, the late marshal's deputies. You can all report to the marshal's office. Someone from my staff will join you there in very short order with your specific assignments. All right? Next, you gentlemen representing the Denver police department and Denver County sheriff's office. I would like you to assemble—"

Longarm had already turned away and was pushing his way through the crowd. Henry was close on his heels as Longarm forced a path for both of them, Smiley and Dutch behind Henry, and the other familiar faces converging now on the door leading out of the U.S. attorney's office.

Jesus, Longarm thought, with this many men to work on the case it should be a snap. They'd just surround Colorado, put every man jack in the state into one big herd, and then start tossing out whoever wasn't guilty. Then they could hang whoever was left in the middle.

Helluva idea, he told himself as he slipped out into the cooler and much fresher air in the hallway of the Federal Building. He was already reaching for a cheroot and match. He figured he needed a smoke to help clear his head after all the pushing and shoving inside that packed room.

But overall, he thought, things were looking pretty good for the lawmen and perilous for the sons of bitches. With this many people on the job and some good solid backing from the powers that be, they should be able to shake the bastards out of the weeds however carefully they might have gone to ground.

Yeah, Longarm decided as he scratched the match head and applied the resulting flame to the tip of his cigar, things were looking pretty good, everything considered.

Chapter 5

"That's just about the dumbest idea I *ever* heard!" Longarm yelped, on his feet and listening to the words come out of his mouth before he had time to think about it.

Not that he likely would have said anything different if he had taken time for thought. What he'd said was the truth plain and simple: This plan *was* the dumbest damn thing he'd ever in his life heard.

The man at the front of the room, a lower-level legal assistant from the U.S. attorney's office named Carl Rakestrom, looked like he wanted to crawl underneath the desk. Hell, Longarm would've approved if he did.

"Look, I . . . I'm just following orders. You know?"

"What I know, dammit, is that this idea is stupid. Dumb. Idiotic. How many ways can I say it?" Longarm snapped at him.

"We all just have to—"

"Like hell we all have to follow orders," Longarm said, cutting Rakestrom off. "Not stupid orders like this. My God, man. You want to put all us old, experienced people on bullshit routine assignments when there's important work to be done? That's crazy, that's what it is."

Longarm could hear a chorus of agreement coming in mumbled undertones from some of the others in the room, notably from Dutch and Henry and Smiley.

"Perhaps I didn't explain it fully," Rakestrom said. The fellow looked quite thoroughly miserable. And so he damn well ought to, Longarm thought, with this sort of moronic message to deliver.

"The thing is," Rakestrom said, trying to back up and start over, "there is no one here to appoint an interim successor to Marshal Vail. Normally that would be the prerogative of the U.S. attorney. But with him gone too, well, there simply isn't anyone capable of making that appointment. Not until Washington comes up with proper instructions. So in the meantime, the marshal's office and all you people will have to work under the direction of Acting U.S. Attorney Cotton.

"And it is his judgment, acting with the advice of others in the office and with certain suggestions from the Secret Service people, that we use you experienced deputies to maintain the normal, everyday functions of the U.S. marshal's office. You know. The serving of writs and warrants, transportation of prisoners, like that. The overall investigation into the slayings of Commissioner Troutman and the others will be under the direct supervisory control of the Secret Service anyway—at the direct order of the president, or so I understand—and they are willing to accept the services of your less-experienced people to assist them in the field." Rakestrom spread his hands and gave Longarm a look of apology, as if perhaps he too thought the decision stupid—but out of his control nonetheless.

"You don't understand," Longarm said, trying to keep his voice calm and low and reasonable, even though he would much rather have raved and snarled and railed at the dumb little son of a bitch. What was he? Twenty years old or thereabouts? All he knew to say was what his ignorant bosses had told him. "This bombing is being blamed on the Utes. Fine. I was there that day. I saw the bomber. It looked like it coulda been a Indian, true. An' maybe some bunch of them was dumb enough to throw that bomb. But that only means the investigation needs to be done by somebody that the Ute people will open up an' talk to. Right? I mean, don't that make sense? An' if I do say so, mister, that means I oughta be the one going out into the field to look into it from that end. The Utes know me. They trust me already. Do you have any idea how difficult it can be to convince an Indian that he oughta trust some stranger? Ask Smiley there. He knows.''

Longarm looked at the tall, saturnine deputy for support. The dour Smiley grimaced once and nodded. "I hate to say it, but Long is right. He already has a foot in the door with those people. Now if it was the Arapaho, that would be different. I know them better. But Long, he knows the Utes. And they know him. The sensible thing would be for Long to pick those of us he wants along to help and then ride south.''

"West,'' Rakestrom corrected. "The Ute reservation, as you apparently do not know, is well to the west from here.''

"South,'' the unsmiling Smiley shot right back at him. "What you an' those fancy-britches popinjays from Washington don't seem to know is that you won't find the Utes on their reservation at this time of year. Not the young, wild ones anyway, and those are the ones Long and us need to talk to about the bombing.''

Rakestrom scowled. "We seem to be getting off the subject,'' he said. "Let me say this one last time. And I'll not hear any further argument. Certain decisions have been reached. It is now up to us, to all of us, to implement those decisions and carry this investigation to a successful conclusion at the earliest possible moment. I have here a list of assignments.'' He held a sheet of paper up for all to see, as if by way of proving something. Longarm had no idea what. "I will announce your assignments, and I expect each of you to carry them out whether you agree with them or not. Is that understood?"

Longarm folded his arms. He wasn't about to give an answer to anything as asinine as this deal seemed to be. And most of the other fellows in the room seemed equally unhappy.

"Long." Rakestrom was looking—glaring was more like it—at Longarm. "You are Long, aren't you?"

"I am," Longarm admitted.

"Albert Morris, charged with tampering with the mails. Are you familiar with the case?"

"I've seen the flyers on him, if that's what you mean."

"Morris has been detained in Salt Lake City. He is being held there waiting formal arrest and transport back here for arraignment and trial. You are detailed to go and get him. See Marshal Vail's clerk for copies of the warrant—one copy for service on the accused and another for the Salt Lake City police, don't forget. You can draw expense vouchers too, of course."

Jesus, Longarm moaned under his breath. Billy Vail was dead. The U.S. attorney was dead. Two important visitors from Washington were dead. And Longarm was supposed to go to Utah to fetch back some petty little asshole who'd clipped somebody else's mail? He could not believe it. Longarm could not fucking *believe* it. Whose idea *was* this anyway?

"Deputy Nathan Krause," Rakestrom's voice droned on, the tone flat and dull and boring. Kind of like his personality, Longarm thought. Without initiative or common sense.

This was, this really and truly had to be, the dumbest damn idea he'd ever heard of. Jesus!

Chapter 6

Longarm was loafing at the back of the room, waiting for the crowd to thin out. He wanted to have a few words with Henry in private. In particular he did not want young Rakestrom around at the time. He was frowning, concentrating on seeing how long an ash he could build at the tip of his cheroot before it fell off, when he felt a touch at his elbow.

"H'lo, Dutch," Longarm said. The man, an old and trusted deputy who had worked for Billy Vail about as long as anybody in the bunch, looked like Hell half warmed over. He needed a haircut, a shave, a bath, and—Longarm's nose wrinkled a mite—a change of clothes. His eyes were crisscrossed with bright scarlet veins. "Hope you don't mind me mentionin' it, Dutch, but you look like you're coming off a three-day drunk."

"Only two days, but you aren't s' wrong after all. I managed to drink enough for three days. Hell, for a week. Ever since I heard the news."

"Yeah, I know what you mean. You, uh . . . I don't recall seeing you at the funeral earlier."

"I wasn't there, Longarm. Billy would've understood. I just couldn't stand it."

"I didn't go out to the cemetery my own self. Same reason."

Dutch nodded and sidled a little closer, lowering his eyes and his voice. "You figure to talk to those boys from the Secret Service, do you?"

"Thought I might have a word with them, yes."

"Don't bother. I just tried it. You know how they introduced themselves? Agent Smith and Agent Jones. Can you believe that shit? They won't even give us their right names, but we're supposed to bow down an' do whatever they say. And invite me in on the investigation? Hell, no. They said they been asked—*asked,* can you believe that—asked to take over for us an' so that's what they'll do. Leave us experienced old-timers to take care o' bullshit while they handle the important work. I never seen any two so slick nor any two so damned arrogant as Mr. Smith an' Mr. Jones. Christ!"

"They said they'd do the important stuff, did they?"

"That isn't the wording they used, but it's damn sure the meaning. They'll handle the investigation into the bombing. Hey, they're the president's own fair-haired boys, right? Us dumb hayseeds can handle the routine garbage. And o' course, when Congress gets its report it'll be the Treasury Department that gets the credit, not Justice."

"I hope whoever replaces Billy isn't a damn politician," Longarm said with feeling.

"I don't think it's gonna make a lick of difference to me who's appointed," Dutch said, his voice bitter. "The son of a bitch won't be able to hold a candle to Billy Vail, I don't care who it is. Me, I'm quitting. Quick as Billy's killer is found, my badge hits the desk. It wouldn't be the same without him."

"I been thinking the same way," Longarm admitted.

"So are you gonna be a good boy an' go serve their stupid papers and all that shit?" Dutch asked.

Longarm grinned. "I always follow orders, Dutch. You know that."

The deputy laughed, the sound short and bitter with no trace of merriment in it. "That's one o' the things I've always admired about you, Longarm."

"You going your own way, Dutch?"

"Just the same as you."

"You got any ideas?"

"Hell, yes, don't we all?"

"If there's anything I can do . . . ," Longarm offered.

"Yeah. The same t' you too. If you need any help with anything, wire Henry. Tell him . . . I dunno, tell him to send you some tulips."

"Dutch. Tulips. Why not."

"I expect to let Henry in on where I am."

"Good idea. I'll do the same." Longarm thought for a moment, then sniggered. "If you need me for anything, ask for some shorts. He can relay the message an' tell me where to find you."

"Fair enough."

Longarm nodded toward the front of the room, toward where Henry was waiting to hand out paperwork to the appropriate parties. Most of the others had gotten whatever they needed and disappeared by now, although Cotton's toady Rakestrom was still hanging around. Apparently the little weasel was not going to leave until the last details were finished. The hell with him, Longarm thought. He'd waited long enough. "Let's take care of this business first," he said to Dutch, "then invite ol' Henry down the street for a drink so we can have a little talk with him in private. You know he'll go along with what you got in mind. He was closer to Billy than any of us."

Dutch grunted an acknowledgment and trailed along behind Longarm.

When Longarm got to the desk, he calmly and quite meekly asked Henry for copies of the warrant charging

Albert Morris with mail tampering. Rakestrom actually smiled at Longarm's obvious acquiescence.

"Thanks," Longarm said, folding the warrants and tucking them safely away. "One thing, though. Instead of regular expense vouchers, I better have some cash outa the petty cash fund. You know how bad some of those Mormons are about honoring U.S. government paper."

Henry didn't bat an eye, even though he knew as well as Longarm did that there probably was not a more law-abiding bunch in the country than Brigham Young's followers over in Utah. Well, when it came to papers and such as that anyway. There were certain aspects of the law that they cheerfully ignored, but that was neither here nor there. No deputy had ever had difficulty securing lodging, transportation, or any other thing in Mormon-controlled territory. But while Longarm knew that, and Henry knew that, and Dutch most assuredly would know that too, Carl Rakestrom would be most unlikely to know it. And that was what counted.

"Of course, Deputy," Henry said. "Two hundred should do you. If you will sign this receipt, please."

"Uh-huh." Longarm accepted a pen from Henry and signed the receipt while Henry unlocked a small cash box and produced a carefully counted sheaf of currency that he then exchanged for the receipt.

Normal procedure called for receipts to be turned in later to account for the use of cash disbursements, but this time, for the first time ever, Henry issued no reminder about that practice.

But then the whole idea here, as Henry would fully understand, was that Longarm wanted to avoid leaving any trail of paper that would indicate where he was and what he was up to.

Hey, he was on his way to Salt Lake City to collect a prisoner. Right? Of course he was.

"Say, I almost forgot something, Henry."

"Yes?"

"You remember that young fella that comes in here every couple months to put a job application on file? The one that wants so awful bad to become a U.S. deputy marshal?"

"Sure. Lenny Harris."

"That's his name, b'damn. Funny how I couldn't remember it."

"You need him?" Henry asked.

"Kinda. I promised to have a drink with him at Tom's Tomcat Saloon this weekend, and I gotta tell him I won't be able to make it, that I have to go to Salt Lake instead."

"He's been working part-time as a night-shift patrolman for Ed Timmons over in Aurora. I expect you can find him there."

"Thanks." Longarm stepped aside and tucked his expense money away while Dutch took care of the paperwork for his piece-of-shit assignment. Then the two of them, Dutch and Longarm, invited Henry to join them for a drink.

"D'you wanta come with us, Rakestrom?" Longarm asked.

The young lawyer blushed a little, confirming—as if confirmation were necessary—that he'd been there for the purpose of eavesdropping. "No, certainly not. I, uh, that is to say, the interim U.S. attorney and I, all of us, appreciate your cooperative attitudes, difficult though this must be for you."

"Yeah, sure," Longarm said, turning his back on the asshole. "Get your hat an' let's go, Henry. I got a taste in my mouth that only some first-rate rye whiskey will wash out."

Chapter 7

Leonard Harris was in the Aurora police station, a badge prominently displayed on his shirtfront and a revolver dangling from his belt that looked to be about half as big as he was, Lenny not being an overlarge specimen of human being. Longarm wasn't sure without asking for a closer look—which he didn't care enough to bother with—but he thought the gun was probably one of those ancient four-pound Walker Colts, originally a cap-and-ball design. This one had been converted to one of the .44 rimfire calibers. Longarm hadn't seen one of those old crocks in years and years.

The part-time night patrolman jumped to his feet when he saw the approach of one of his idols. The youngster wanted desperately to become a U.S. deputy marshal himself, and thought the men who already held such exalted office to be head and shoulders above any other lawmen. As the late Billy Vail's top deputy, Custis Long would be seen by Harris as the cream of the cream. There was a Frenchified expression for that, Longarm knew, but he couldn't remember what it was. He nodded to Harris, who was redheaded, smooth-cheeked, and looked to be fourteen or thereabouts, even though Longarm knew the kid had to be at least twenty-one even to fill out a job application for the Marshals Service.

"Hello, Lenny," Longarm said. The youngster beamed, obviously delighted that one of his heroes actually knew him by name. "You about to make your rounds, are you?"

"I'm not due to go out again for another half hour or so."

Longarm glanced across the room toward where the night sergeant—a man named Edwards, he thought—was sitting with his feet propped up and a magazine open in his lap. "If you was to make your rounds now," Longarm said, "I'd walk along with you."

"Really? I'd like that, sir. I surely would," Harris enthused.

"Come along then, kid."

"Just let me get my hat. Tony, I'm going out now. I'll be back in an hour or so."

"Mind you check the back of Jenkins's store, boy," Edwards said without looking up from his reading. "He claims some kids been sneaking in and stealing candy from him."

"His own kid is more like it," Lenny snorted.

"I know, but I told him we'd keep an eye on his place, so do it, okay?"

"Sure." Lenny grinned and tugged his hat down tight over his ears. "This way, Marshal."

"Longarm," Longarm corrected. "My friends call me Longarm."

Lenny acted as pleased as a pup with a new bone. He squared his shoulders and puffed his chest out and proudly led the way outside and around back of the city hall to begin the process of checking all the storefronts and alleys in the business district.

"Were you wanting a word with me in private, Mar . . . I mean, Longarm?" Harris asked when they were a couple blocks away from Edwards and the police station.

29

"Uh-huh. Got a proposition for you, son. A way you can help me out if you're interested."

"Help you? Honest?"

"It would mean accepting a temporary appointment as a special U.S. deputy marshal and going out on a case unsupervised. Do you think you could handle that?" Longarm asked.

"You aren't funning me, are you, sir?"

"No, Harris, I'm serious as I can be. I'm sure you understand how busy we all are, what with the marshal and those other folks being blown up by that bomb and everything."

"Yes, sir. I mean, I would of been at the funeral myself today but I had to get ready to come on duty here tonight."

"The thing is, I need some help. Can you get off for a few days?"

"Yes, *sir*," Harris said instantly. "You just tell me what you want, and I'll do it."

Longarm brought out the warrants he'd gotten from Henry that afternoon and explained to Harris what they were and how—and where—they should be served.

"All the way to Salt Lake City? Wow!"

Longarm had the distinct impression that Lenny Harris had never been that far from home his whole life long. And that he was plenty excited now at the prospect of being sent off on a genuine assignment as a U.S. deputy marshal to such a distant and exotic place.

"You'll do it?" Longarm asked.

"You bet I will, sir. I mean . . . Longarm." If Lenny's grin got any bigger, Longarm figured his face might break in two.

"Here's a hundred dollars cash. That should be enough to cover expenses getting there and back for you and the prisoner. Do you have handcuffs?"

"Yes, sir, of course."

"Leg irons?"

"No, I don't have none of those."

"Here. I brought a pair. Here's the keys. I don't expect you to have any trouble with your prisoner, but don't take any chances."

"No, sir, I won't."

"Keep your receipts so you can turn them over to me when you get back. Here's a badge you'll be authorized to carry."

Lenny looked so proud, Longarm was afraid the kid might burst plumb open at the seams.

"Now raise your right hand, son, an' repeat after me. . . ."

The oath—such as it was—Longarm made up as he went along. Whatever the words, they would satisfy Lenny Harris. And Longarm hoped nobody else would ever ask about this. Or so much as know about it—with the possible exception someday of Henry. Longarm might choose to tell him. Or not.

And hell, for all Longarm knew, this deputation business might actually prove to be legal and binding if push ever came to shove. After all, he did have the authority to deputize posse members and the like under certain circumstances. And if he hadn't inquired too closely about those circumstances and whether this business with young Harris might fit under them, well, that would only be necessary in the unlikely event that something drew official attention to the arrangement.

In the meantime, though—and that was the important thing—in the meantime Deputy Marshal Long was now free to do what he thought properly had to be done.

Chapter 8

Longarm left the Denver & Rio Grande at the Colorado Springs station, and immediately looked for a streetcar to take him over to Colorado City, even though it probably would have been more convenient to hire a horse right there in Colorado Springs and get on with things.

His only reason for doing it the way he did was that he just plain felt more comfortable in Colorado City than he ever managed to do in Colorado Springs. The difference, he supposed, was easy enough to understand. In Colorado Springs there were a reported twenty-odd churches, though he hadn't actually gone around and counted. And by force of law not one single solitary saloon. The serving of liquor to the great unwashed was strictly illegal in the hoity-toity city where the Eastern swells and the newly rich hung out. Although, as Longarm had reason to know, rich folks got just as drunk as anybody when they were safely in private, with only their own grand kind around to see.

Good old Colorado City, on the other hand, was loud, raunchy, boisterous, and full of both good humor and bad whiskey. Or sometimes the other way around, but that was all right too.

Anyway, Longarm's preference, now and pretty much

any time that duty permitted, was to spend his time and do his business with the honest—or mostly so—burghers of Colorado City in preference to their neighbors just a couple miles to the east of that much older community.

He let the horse-drawn car on rails carry him past the bustle of Colorado City's business district and two blocks on toward Manitou, picked up his saddle and carpetbag, and swung down off the streetcar without bothering to ask for a stop.

The air was crisp there, higher and cooler and cleaner than it was back in Denver, with less smoke and soot and smell in it. It felt good in a man's lungs, and Longarm always found himself breathing deeper and standing taller when he was outside the stink of the big city. He shouldered his gear and began walking toward a livery he'd done business with several times in the past and where he knew he could count on finding a square deal.

"Two horses, Marshal? How come two?" the hostler asked when Longarm told the man what he required.

"One to fork, Jerry, and one to pack. An' I'll need a pack frame and fixings to go on the spare. Cheroot? These are good'uns." He smiled and held out a pair of the slim, dark smokes. The hostler selected one and Longarm took the other, striking a match and lighting both of the mild and flavorful cigars.

"You're wanting a favor, ain't you?" the man named Jerry said with a grin, obviously taking no offense to the notion but a trifle cautious nonetheless.

"Am I that obvious about it?"

"After giving me one of these expensive smokes, me as hasn't tasted anything this tender since I last had a virgin? Yeah, Marshal, I'd say you're being pretty obvious."

Longarm chuckled. "It's true. The thing is, the price of these is coming outa my own pocket. It won't be on the usual voucher." Which was true enough, or would be in the long run. Longarm expected his expenses on this trip to exceed the hundred dollars he still had in his pocket from what Henry had advanced him, and anything over that would surely have to come straight out of Longarm's own meager bank account.

Not that he begrudged the spending. Far from it. If this case beggared him and took everything he could expect to make in the next twenty years to boot, it would be well worth the while just so he could come face-to-face with the sons of bitches who'd killed Billy Vail. This was one time when money didn't matter. Not money nor fairness nor law nor much of anything else, except that he succeed. Billy Vail's murderers *would* be brought to justice. To court if that proved convenient, but to justice of a certainty. Longarm figured to see to that.

Jerry raised an eyebrow, but when Longarm failed to offer any explanations, the hostler did not press him about it. "All right. I'll cut you a deal. You've done business here before, and I expect you will again in the future."

"Count on it, my friend," Longarm promised.

Jerry nodded. "Come along. If you'll trust my judgment, I'll pick out the best I've got for you."

"Trot 'em out and tack 'em up, Jerry, for I got work to do and damn-all time to do it in," Longarm said, sucking pale smoke deep into his lungs, then quickly stubbing out the coal on his cheroot before he followed Jerry inside the livery barn.

Chapter 9

"I'll take those. And those there, all you got of them. Is that toilet water in those fancy little bottles? Good, I'll take . . . I dunno . . . how many you got of those? Fine, I'll take 'em all. What about hairpins? I'll need a couple pounds of hairpins. An' sewing needles. Thirty, maybe forty papers of pins. All right, I think that takes care of about everything I need in this area. Now let's look over here." Longarm stalked through the mercantile, picking and pointing this way and that.

"Alcohol," he said. "I need some alcohol. What d'you have, two-gallon casks? I'll take four of 'em. An' molasses. About two gallons of that. Let's see . . . some caramel coloring. For sure I want some caramel coloring. What else? Pepper. And salt, of course. Sugar. Say, fifty pounds . . . no, never mind the sugar. I think I'm building too heavy a load here. Forget the sugar an' the salt. But I still need some pepper. Two pound of it. And tobacco. Got to have some tobacco. Ten pounds . . . no, make it twenty. Might as well do this right. How much have I spent here so far?"

The storekeeper bent over the notepad he'd been scribbling on and made some calculations. "Sixty-four dollars and, um, twenty cents. We'll round that down to sixty-four dollars even," he said in an outpouring of generosity.

"All right," Longarm told him. "One last thing then. I'll need some of these cheroots. You got them in stock?"

"Sure thing."

"Give me twenty of them, please."

"That will be everything?"

"I reckon it will have to do." It was either that or go back to the livery and hire another packhorse, Longarm knew. Besides, this one load would use up just about all his available cash. He made a mental note to find a bank when he left the mercantile. Maybe between him and his badge he could convince someone there to honor a draft against his account in Denver. He hoped so.

"I'll have my boy package everything for you and bring it out to your horse," the storekeeper said. "In the meantime, if you don't mind, I have a few errands to run. Would that be all right?"

"Sure, mister. I reckon your boy can handle the rest of it." Longarm paid the man for his purchases and stood idling about the store while the storekeeper disappeared briefly into his back room, then emerged once more to remove his apron and put on a suit coat and narrow-brimmed hat before going out onto the street.

The boy, a fat kid in his teens with approximately equal amounts of pimples and peach fuzz on his cheeks, came out and began assembling Longarm's purchases into small bundles suitable for lashing onto a crossbuck packsaddle.

"Let me know when you're ready with all that," Longarm told him. "I'll want to do the actual packing my own self." He knew better than to allow a stranger, any stranger, to make up a pack. Some people just never could get the hang of making up a proper pack. In fact, Longarm suspected, most people wouldn't know how to make up a balanced, durable load, and anything less than correct was a certain-sure recipe for trouble.

"Five minutes, mister."

"That'll be fine, son." Longarm stepped outside to wait on the sidewalk out in the clean, fresh air and sunshine.

He wasn't out there alone for very long, for within a minute or so the storekeeper hustled past, and practically treading on the man's heels, a fellow wearing a soiled blue coat with copper buttons on it and a black-beaked blue cap, with a six-pointed star prominent on his chest, confronted Longarm.

"Afternoon, Officer," Longarm said. He reached into his pocket for a cheroot, and couldn't help but notice that the policeman flinched when he did so, then visibly relaxed when Longarm's hand came out with nothing more threatening than the cigar. "Is something wrong?"

"Could be. For openers, I want you to keep your hands well clear of that pistol on your belly."

"That sounds reasonable," Longarm said mildly. "Just to let you know, I'm fixing to reach into my vest pocket here for a match. Is that all right?"

The policeman nodded. "Do it then, but slow."

Longarm shrugged, got his match, and thumbed it aflame. He took his time building a decent coal on the cheroot before he shook the match out and flicked it into the street. He was not feeling especially inclined to offer the copper a smoke. "So what's on your mind, Officer?"

"You've been buying the makings of trade whiskey," the policeman said.

"That's right. Anything wrong with that?"

"You've also been buying trade goods for Indians."

"Is that a fact?"

"You know it is."

"No, sir, what I *know*—as opposed to what I might or might not surmise if our situations was reversed—is that I've bought a bunch of goods that are every one

37

legal to sell an' legal to own. Beyond that, friend, you're only guessing.''

''Don't sass me, mister, or I'll have your ass behind bars so fast you won't know what hit you.''

Longarm smiled. But there was no trace of warmth in the expression. ''Is that a fact now?''

''Damn right it is. You're intending to sell whiskey to some Indians. That's against the law.''

''Is it really?''

''You know it is as well as I do. That's a federal law, mister. You can't sell whiskey to Indians.''

''You know something about federal law, do you?''

''Everybody knows about that federal law.''

Longarm pursed his lips in thought for a moment, then nodded and blew a thin stream of smoke. Direct into the copper's smug face.

''I'm warning you. . . .''

''Real big on warnings, ain't you?'' Longarm offered.

''If it's trouble you're looking for, I can damn sure give it to you.'' The cop backed away two steps and put his hand on the saw-handle butt of a large, somewhat rusty revolver at his waist.

''Before you pull that thing an' get yourself shot full of holes,'' Longarm said, ''I wanta show you something. But I got to reach inside my coat to get at it.''

''Keep your hands right where they are, damn you,'' the policeman croaked, his voice tight and hoarse with fear. Sweat beaded his forehead and trickled out of the headband on his cap.

''I am a federal officer,'' Longarm told him, ''and I do not have any desire to start anything with you, friend. But I damn sure do not intend to stand here an' let you get crazy.''

''You're a liar is what you are,'' the copper responded. ''You're a whiskey runner and God knows what else, and I'm taking you in. Now turn around and put your hands behind your back so's I can cuff you.''

Longarm thought about it. He did not want to shoot the man. After all, his only offense was that he was an asshole. And if you once started trying to wipe out all the assholes you encountered, why, you'd hardly know where to start nor how to finish. Still, Longarm did not think he could trust this fella to restrain himself, even if—or especially if—he ever had Longarm in irons.

"I have a better idea," Longarm said, taking his cheroot out of his mouth and giving it a critical inspection. "Just a second." Longarm reached again into his vest pocket. But a different vest pocket this time. He came out not with a match, but with the brass-framed little .44 derringer he carried there.

"What we seem to have here," Longarm said, "is a Mexican standoff. Sort of. So whyn't you take your hand off the grip of that hogleg—unless you think you can draw an' fire quick before I have time to pull this trigger—an' then I'll show you my credentials, because y'see, I really am a United States deputy marshal an' if I get any more pissed off at you, friend, you're the one going behind bars. On a charge of obstructing a federal officer in the pursuit of his duties. Do we understand each other? I hope we do."

The policeman's eyes had gotten so wide they practically bulged clean out of his skull, and the sweat was pouring off him now.

"Please," Longarm urged.

The cop nodded, his face gone white with fear, and carefully held his hand well clear of the butt of his revolver.

"Thanks," Longarm said. "Now let me offer you a cheroot, friend, whilst you look over my badge an' stuff." Still holding the derringer, he reached inside his coat. He had never gotten around to cocking the small but viciously effective little weapon; after all, he hadn't wanted to risk an accident if the Colorado City policeman did anything truly stupid like try to jump him.

Chapter 10

Longarm couldn't believe he'd done that. It was stupid. Worse than stupid. It wasn't like him to make dumb plays like that. For crying out loud . . . taking out a gun and waving it around at a local copper. Jeez, he wouldn't have so much as had grounds for complaint if some local Good Samaritan had come along and backshot him in an effort to help the copper out of a jam. Like, for instance, the storekeeper who'd turned him in to the police. Of course the man had done that. He was being a good citizen, that was all, reporting what he figured was a crime about to happen.

Hell, Longarm practically deserved the whole thing. For sure he knew better than to act like a crazed kid. He could have taken time to go to the damn jail with the policeman and establish his bona fides there. It wasn't like there was any huge urgency for action here. Billy Vail was dead and gone. Nothing was going to change that. And no passage of time, not years and not decades, would keep Longarm and the other boys from hunting down and finding every last son of a bitch who had anything to do with the assassinations. Longarm decided he needed to put the damn brakes on and start thinking like a grown-up instead of charging off with his head up his ass.

Besides, it was uncomfortable as hell trying to ride a horse when your head was firmly socketed in your own ignorant backside.

Still, whether he deserved the break or not, he'd gotten away with his stupidity and no real harm had been done. Maybe it would even prove to be helpful if it taught him a lesson. To slow down and pay attention to the business at hand. Don't demand instant justice, but let it come in its own time. And then savor it like the smoke from a particularly fine cigar.

Longarm reined his rented horse south away from Colorado City, down along the base of the Front Range foothills, the stoutly made packhorse trailing amiably along at the end of its lead rope. He was a good three or four miles south of town by the time he remembered that in his annoyance with himself he'd clean forgotten to go to the bank to get some more cash. Still, there were other banks in other towns. And he wouldn't likely need any cash money again until he got to another town. It wasn't worth turning back for.

He found the trail he wanted easily enough. He'd been there before a couple times in the past. He turned west then, the trail commencing to climb in a zigzag route of switchbacks and rises, toward the heavy, looming shoulder of the mountain they called Cheyenne. Although why it was named for the Cheyenne tribe when it was the Utes who came there to summer on its flanks each year, he had never quite understood.

Further to the west and a bit north by now, he knew, there was the much more impressive presence of Pikes Peak, but from this close to the mountains Longarm could no longer see the mantle of deep snow that capped this highest and most magnificent peak in the range that started on the grassy plains and leaped with spectacular suddenness toward the clouds.

From where Longarm now rode it was Cheyenne Mountain that filled the horizon and warned travelers away with its size and the steepness of its slopes. Anyone who did not know the mountain would look at it from afar and quickly conclude that the mountain was unscalable, or that at best it would take a man with ropes and special climbing skills to reach its summit. The truth, though, for those who knew the mountain's secrets, was that this—and nearly the whole of the range for scores of miles in either direction—was crosshatched with narrow, often precipitous trails that the Ute tribes had followed for . . . who knows how long? Perhaps hundreds upon hundreds of years in their annual migrations between the mountains and the plains.

The eastern-dwelling bands of Utes eschewed the white man's practice of summering high and wintering in lowlands. Instead the Indians had long ago learned to descend to the grasslands in summer in order to find the great herds of buffalo that were the mainstay of their culture, then in winter retreat into the mountains, where they would remain safe from any approach by enemy raiders, locked snug and comfortable behind snowclogged passes while their many enemies were left far behind and below on the warmer plains.

Longarm had been privileged to travel in the company of the Utes on several occasions in the past, and while he could not claim to truly know the trails, he at least was aware of them, and he figured he could puzzle out a way that would bring him soon to wherever the tribe was now. For if they were not yet camped on the lower flanks of Cheyenne Mountain, they were sure to be on their way there. Longarm figured to intercept them. And to talk to them.

If they or any other band of Utes was involved in the assassination plot against the commissioner, a plot that had killed more than merely the Washington City politician and his lady, Longarm believed he would surely get a whiff of it from old friends in the tribe.

And once he had the scent, he would not let it be. Longarm swore that silently to himself. And to the memory of Billy Vail.

Chapter 11

He spent the night high on the slopes of Cheyenne Mountain, the lights of the plains towns clearly visible below him in the thin, clean air. There was Colorado City to the north, and Colorado Springs east of it, Fountain straight east from where Longarm was, and far to the south, a faint glimmer that probably was distant Pueblo. From this elevation Longarm figured he could see a hundred miles out across the grass, maybe further. Manitou would be there somewhere too, to the north of him, but from the location he'd picked for a campsite it was not visible.

Something else not visible, and something he'd hoped to see, was the rising plumes of smoke that would have marked the Ute encampment.

The Indians just hadn't gotten this far yet, dammit, although he was pretty sure they normally should have been on Cheyenne or somewhere close to it by this time of year. He couldn't help but wonder if there had been something that had distracted them from their ordinary pursuits this year. Something like planning the assassination of the special commissioner who was capable of taking away from them the grazing rights on their own land.

For that was certainly the appearance of things. After all, Longarm had with his own eyes seen the cape-shrouded back of the assassin's head. And the hair he'd seen, long and black and ropy with grease, for damn sure wasn't any white man's hair.

He had to admit the possibility that some of the hotter-tempered young warriors among the Utes might have planned it.

They would have known about the commissioner's arrival. It hadn't been any secret. The Indian agent would have told them all about it. Would have warned them of the dangers if the commissioner chose to rule against them when he reported back to Congress and the president.

And in truth there wasn't much reason why the Utes, or for that matter any of the wild tribes, should place unbounded trust in the politicians from back in Washington. The government's past record wasn't exactly worth much in the way of bragging rights when it came to upholding land agreements, even those guaranteed by solemn treaty. When there was a hunger for land on the part of citizens—voting citizens—then it was the Indian who generally had to accept the inevitable and settle for less than he'd thought he was getting the first time the cards were dealt. Or the second.

That wasn't a pleasant thing to contemplate. But it was true. Longarm couldn't deny it. And the Utes would certainly recognize it as well as anybody. They were not, after all, a stupid people, nor at this point even an uneducated one. Enough of their young men had been sent east to the school at Carlisle, or south to Santa Fe, to study and learn and report back about all the things they'd seen and read. Enough, for that matter, had studied white ways and white books and white politics in their own agency schools so that few of them could now-adays be considered untutored savages. The young in particular were aware of and informed about the world around them, and they would understand the realities of what they faced now that the white livestock growers, cattlemen and sheep men alike, coveted the Ute grazing lands.

Was that enough to cause an explosion of emotions strong enough to carry Billy away?

That was one of the things Longarm had to determine.

That was why he was there now instead of being over in Utah where he'd been assigned.

Longarm pondered and fretted far into the night before he finally closed his eyes and managed some sleep.

Come the dawn, he was already descending the southwest shoulder of Cheyenne Mountain into a notch that separated it from the next lumpy peak—the name of which Longarm couldn't call to mind—and then again began to climb.

By late morning he was crossing a high, almost flat divide, sunshine making the bright-gleaming snowcap on Pikes Peak almost hurtful to the eye. Before him the north-south-running peaks and ranges ran on and on to the west like so many waves marching across the ocean surface. Except these waves were carved of solid rock and rose many thousands of feet into the sky.

Longarm wasn't sure, but he guessed he was at eleven, maybe twelve thousand feet of elevation there. He could feel the thinness of the chill air in his lungs, and he slowed his pace lest the lowland-raised horses take sick on him. He'd known horses to die at these high elevations, just go into hard sweats and then lie down and die for no other apparent reason, and he did not especially want to find himself afoot up there. There was no particular danger, of course, but the loss of the time it would take to walk out would damn sure be a bother, to say nothing about having to leave all his gifts behind.

He stopped for an early lunch at the top of a talus chute, a narrow gap that descended at an appallingly steep angle for at least three hundred feet into the next valley.

The chute was not rump-sliding steep. But it didn't miss it by a hell of a lot. It was bad enough that normally he would have looked for an alternate way down off the peak, but the only trail in sight dropped faithfully into the scree there. And if both game and Indians took it for the easiest path, Longarm wasn't going to argue the point.

He let the horses rest before tackling it, then checked and tightened his cinches before starting down. Even so, he got a scare about halfway down when his damn front cinch slipped and he found himself riding the neck of the rented horse with nothing but the animal's ears in front of his pommel.

The horse was steady, thank goodness. A fall onto the rocks and small boulders that filled the chute there would have been a bitch at best, and quite possibly could have spelled disaster. Longarm dropped off without spooking the horse into a misstep, set the saddle once again—even tighter this time; he supposed the damn horse had puffed its belly full of air the last time—and made it the rest of the way down without incident.

Picking his trail from several that fanned out from the bottom of the rocky chute, he made his way out of the rocks and aspen groves onto rolling hills covered with thin, coarse, high-altitude bunchgrasses, then into a broad, shallow bowl that looked like the mouth of an ancient volcano. And probably was.

A narrow stream meandered out of the west side of the bowl and down toward a broad, spring-green basin that Longarm could see beyond and below the dense pine forests that covered the slopes now that the elevation was diminishing a mite.

At one point, when he splashed through the creek for the twentieth time or thereabouts, crisscrossing back and forth to hold to the easiest path, his horse stopped to grab a mouthful of cold water. Longarm leaned down from his saddle to help himself to a handful of it too, and was amused to see the bright glint of purest gold sparkle up at him from a dozen points or more on the creek bed at his feet. Gold. A newcomer to the country would have gone wild at the sight. But then Longarm wasn't a newcomer. And these mountain streams were full of the iron pyrites known—quite rightly—as fool's gold. He settled for the drink of water and left the "gold dust" where it was.

Another few miles and the trail crossed an open hump, giving him a view of the land spread out below. More miles to the northwest he could see smoke. Several plumes of smoke rising into the sky. Finally, he thought, riding on, this time with a destination he could aim for.

Chapter 12

"Dammit," Longarm snapped out loud even though the only living things anywhere close enough to hear were the horses. The plumes of smoke he'd seen from up on the mountain were not a Ute camp but a collection of log cabins, a white settlement way the hell and gone up there. He even recognized the place. Damn if he hadn't been there before. But he'd never approached from this direction before, which was why he hadn't realized how close he had come.

He could not immediately recall the name of the place, but as he got closer he could see a sign nailed over the front door of the largest and most centrally located structure: "United States Post Office, Florissant, Colorado." The wording was off center, and behind the word "Colorado" he could see where the additional word "Territory" had been scratched off sometime after Colorado was granted statehood. The place had been there for some time, obviously.

And yeah, he had been before. Stopped at least once that he could recall, and passed through another couple of times. The settlement had been built on the major roadway linking Colorado City with Fairplay and a number of other mining communities on the far side of South Park. There still was no railroad here, although one was talked of from time to time, mostly due to the amount of commerce over the highway. Down in Colorado City there were a number of manufacturers of mining equipment, and of course there were customers for the fabricated goods over west in the mining camps. That sort of arrangement generally led at least to the cutting of roadways, as it had here, and sometimes as well to quicker and more effective means of hauling heavy equipment like the boilers and hoists and things made down below.

Longarm remembered that now. But he sure hadn't realized how far north he'd angled after crossing south of Pikes Peak.

He didn't have any particular need of a store at the moment, having stocked up down in Colorado City before he left there, but the thought of coffee and cooking other than his own was always welcome. Besides, someone here might well know where he could find the late-traveling Utes.

Longarm tied his horses and swung down onto the dark red, gravel-filled soil. He had been in the saddle steady for some hours, and it felt good to move around now. He took out a cheroot and lighted it, then stepped inside the building.

"Hello, Marshal."

Longarm blinked. The man behind the counter looked vaguely familiar, but Longarm sure as hell could not put a name to him. "I'm sorry, but I. . . ."

The Florissant postmaster grinned. "Bob Giver," he said.

"Sure, I remember now, Bob," Longarm lied. "Nice to see you again." Giver offered a hand, and Longarm shook it.

"You up here to arrest somebody, are you?"

"Oh, no, nothing exciting like that. Trying to find the

50

dang Utes. They aren't down yet, though they normally would be by now.''

"Nothing serious, I hope," Giver said.

"Naw, nothing serious." Murder, bombing, stuff like that. Nothing serious.

Giver peered off into the distance as if there was something in a far corner of the roof that would give him the powers of insight. Or something. After a moment he shook his head. "I'm not for sure where they'd be either. Used to come by here every year before now, but they quit using the road a couple years back after that bunch of young bucks ran wild and killed those fellows down the other side of the Divide."

Longarm remembered reading about that, although he hadn't been involved in any investigation that might have taken place afterward. A bunch of young Ute warriors who had never proven themselves in a fight decided one night to claim their manhood by way of taking some scalps. They slipped away from the rest of the band and found a pair of out-of-work mining men camped out beside the highway, jumped and killed them, and took their scalps to dance with. It had made quite a stir in the newspapers at the time, but that was half a dozen years ago or longer. As far as Longarm could tell, that was the last time these eastern Utes had killed anyone. "I remember that," he said, accurately this time.

"So do others around here. Made it pretty clear the savages weren't to use the road anymore." Giver shrugged. "It cost me a little business, but not so much. They never did all that much trade with me anyway when they came through."

"You don't happen to know what route they follow nowadays?" Longarm asked.

"Sure do. They come down Slater Creek—that's south of here about twelve, fourteen miles—then up and over the backside of the Peak."

Longarm grunted. That was pretty much the way he'd just now come. Without running into the band he was looking for.

"They'll be along by and by," Giver said. "I've never known them to fail. They always come eventually."

"Guess I'll ride back down and see can I find them."

"Anything I can do for you while you're here, Marshal?"

"Not unless you got something to eat."

"No, but if you're riding south you'll pass by the Widow Clark's place. She sets a good table and won't charge you for it, although if you insist, she'll take a little something to replace the supplies she's used up. It, uh . . . she could use the help, if you see what I mean."

"I do, and I thank you for the suggestion." Longarm touched the brim of his Stetson, then turned away. He stopped again, though, before he reached the door and turned back to face Giver once more. "Say, now. Would you happen to have a piece of paper and a stamp? It just now occurred to me that I took off from Denver without leaving word, and I oughta do something about that while I can."

"Paper, envelope, and stamp, all for five cents. You can't find a better bargain than that," Giver claimed. "Oh, and a pen and ink to write your letter with. You can stand right here at the counter if you like. I won't peek, not even after you leave."

Longarm pushed his hat back a mite and accepted the writing implements Giver laid out for him. In all the fuss and feathers after Billy's murder, he never had gotten around to telling Debbie what was going on. She deserved better than that. Especially, Longarm thought, if he intended to see her once he got back to the city.

And he damn sure did hope to see that lovely lady

again once things shook out and Billy's murderer was where he properly belonged.

Longarm paused for a moment of thought, then began scratching a quick note for the tall and buxom nurse whose company he enjoyed so much.

Chapter 13

The postmaster's directions were easy to follow, and
even—wonder of wonders—accurate. Longarm found
the broad, grassy valley twelve or fourteen miles south
of the Florissant Post Office where one creek flowing
sluggishly out of the west joined another, faster-moving
stream that came down from the north. Longarm suspected that the north-south-flowing creek was the same
one he'd already crossed a dozen or more times when
he was up on the mountain. Here the two joined to continue southward, no doubt eventually adding their waters
to the Arkansas River.

It was not the creeks that captured Longarm's attention, though, so much as it was the numerous fire rings
left unused at least over the past winter, and the elliptical
beaten areas of grass, covering an area of four or five
acres nearby, that showed where temporary lodges had
been erected in past years.

This, he was sure, was one of the Utes' stopping
places on their twice-annual migrations from the mountains to the plains and back again.

He was equally sure that the tribe had not yet gotten
this far in their journey this season.

Longarm spent several minutes gazing out over the

landscape, trying to decide if he should ride west up the narrow, lush valley of what the Florissant postmaster called Slater Creek, or if he should instead venture south into the area sometimes known as High Park, the smallest and least known of the chain of protected wintering places.

A wrong choice could mean missing the tribe in their travel and a serious delay in the pursuit of Billy Vail's murderer or murderers.

After a few minutes of thought, he accepted logic above urgency and stepped down from his saddle to begin unpacking. Since he did not know which direction to take from there, it made sense to sit still and wait for the Utes to come to him.

"Well, I'll be a son of a bitch," Longarm mumbled under his breath as a soft, crunching-tearing sound wakened him from what had been a deep sleep. It was not quite dawn yet, the sky to the east pale and luminous, but with no sign yet of actual sunlight visible beyond the tall, conical peak that dominated the horizon above the valley.

The source of the noise that had disturbed him, Longarm discovered without having to move from his bed, was a herd of elk cropping grass on the far side of the creek not forty yards from where he'd spread his bedroll.

There must have been well over a hundred animals in all strung out beside the creek bed, twenty-five or thirty of them bunched close enough to hit with a well-pitched rock. They obviously had come down to water in the thin light of dawn and were taking their time about it, enjoying the rich bottomland grass as well.

Longarm looked them over and decided they were too grand a gift to be ignored. After all, what is a party without plenty of roast meat for the feasting?

And Longarm did intend to throw a party for the Utes when they showed up.

With a grunt of satisfaction he slid the Winchester out of its scabbard and, still lying snug and warm inside his blankets, took easy aim on the chest cavity of a particularly large and tasty-looking cow.

The herd erupted into a miniature earthquake of snorts and whistled warning calls and pounding hoofs at the sound of Longarm's gunshot, but the cow dropped in her tracks and never so much as quivered, while the rest of the bunch ran frantically toward the line of low hills to the east, where they immediately disappeared into the timber. Longarm never got another glimpse of them climbing for the safety of the heights, even though he knew where to watch, where the huge, majestic animals almost had to be. Within seconds he might have believed he'd imagined the whole thing. Except, that is, for the presence of the dead cow lying on the grass mere paces from his bed.

Stretching then and yawning, Longarm laid the Winchester aside, sat up, and pushed the covers off his body. He leaned down to stir last night's ashes into this morning's fire with the addition first of some dry grass and then, quickly after, a handful of twigs and small branches he'd gathered the evening before. As soon as he had a fire going, he set his coffeepot over it and only then stood, yawning again, to bring out his knife and walk over to the downed elk.

He had work to do there so he would be ready when the Utes arrived.

Chapter 14

"Long Arm! Heya. Long time no see, yes?"

"Too long, old friend," Longarm told the grinning, nearly toothless Indian who dropped unhurriedly off the side of his horse and came forward to grab Longarm in a bear hug that made rib cartilage pop. "How are you, Bad Eye?"

"Good, yes, and you, Long Arm?"

"Better now that I see my friends the Ute people."

"You come to visit with your friends, Long Arm?"

"I do, Bad Eye. Tell your women there is meat to roast, there, and tonight when the meat is ready to eat we will feast together."

"You have whiskey, Long Arm?" Bad Eye asked, eyeing—with two perfectly sharp eyes despite his name—the casks sitting some distance apart from Longarm's spare and spartan camp.

"You know it would be against the law for me to give whiskey to you, Bad Eye. I cannot do that." The Indian's expression became sad. Longarm winked at him. "On the other hand, I can't pay attention to everything that goes on behind my back tonight," he added.

Bad Eye laughed and turned to say something to the group of young warriors who had also dismounted and come over to get a closer look at this white warrior who several times in the past had proven himself a friend of the tribe. The men chortled with delight at whatever it was Bad Eye told them. Not that Longarm had much doubt about the gist of that conversation. There would be whiskey to be had this evening, and best of all, it would be without cost. They would not even have to barter for it, just help themselves whenever Long Arm was not looking.

Longarm let the men talk among themselves. While they did so he was busy searching beyond the gathering of males, peering at the crowd of women and children who pushed and shoved as they jockeyed for positions from which they too could inspect the tall white man.

There was, he admitted to himself, a particular face he hoped to see there.

But he did not. Dammit, he did not. Spotted Fawn must not have come along with this particular band this year. She might have stayed on the reservation far to the west or gone off with another band, or might even be accompanying a husband somewhere for all he knew. After all, it had been a rather long time since he'd seen her.

He'd been hoping, though. He admitted that to himself now. He thought about asking Bad Eye, and then decided it would be better to let it be. If she was not there, well, there was nothing he could do about it. But he'd sure been hoping. . . .

"Come, Long Arm. Smoke with us while the women make the lodges ready and kill some fat dogs to add to your meat. Tonight we will feast together, heya? Tonight we are brothers once more."

"Yes, Bad Eye. Tonight we are brothers again."

Enemies tomorrow perhaps, Longarm acknowledged to himself alone, but brothers tonight.

"Come, Long Arm. My pipe is here. Do you have tobacco?"

Dutifully Longarm pulled out a twist of tobacco and gave it to the headman of the band, not expecting any of it to be returned—nor was he disappointed in that expectation.

But then this exact thing was the reason he'd come all this way to find the Utes. Now he needed to soften them up and make their tongues loose. By morning, he figured, he should have a pretty good idea if any of this bunch—or for that matter any of the rest of the tribe— might have been plotting to kill the commissioner from Washington City.

Chapter 15

Helluva party, Longarm thought with considerable satisfaction. Most of the Utes were sloppy drunk by now. Hell, he was kinda tight his own self. The world had a nice, fuzzy glow and the sounds of many conversations swirled and buzzed all around him.

Longarm sat in a place of honor before a roaring fire, the creek—and the whiskey—behind him where he could not see the frequent forays into the booze made by the young men of the tribe.

The whole thing was, or so he hoped, on the legal side of things. Technically speaking, that is. And that, after all, was what would be important to the lawyers who might someday look into these events should Longarm ever be called upon to testify about what he learned there. Federal law prohibited him from selling or trading whiskey to Indians, even enjoined against giving the stuff away.

But dammit, Longarm wasn't doing any of those things. He was sitting there having a friendly talk while behind his back his friends stole him blind.

More or less. And if the reality was something on the "less" side of that ledger, well, what of it? The important thing right now was to get some tongues oiled to the point that these fellows would open up and talk to him. About grazing rights and white cattlemen. About special commissioners and bombs and shit like that.

But not yet. The Indians weren't up to that quite yet, and neither was Longarm.

He belched and reached for a cheroot, offering one to Bad Eye, and then putting it back in his pocket when the tribal leader's eyes glazed over and the man commenced to take a decided list to starboard, leaning further and further to the side until gravity got the better of equilibrium and Bad Eye toppled over and began to snore.

Longarm snorted and helped himself to another drink of the raw whiskey he'd manufactured with alcohol, creek water, and an assortment of flavorful additives. It wasn't entirely bad stuff if he did say so. And got better and better the more he drank of it.

He searched on the ground for some dried grass that he could use to light his cigar, but when he found what he wanted, prepared it, and leaned forward to hold it in the fire, a small hand appeared in front of him with an already flaming twist. Longarm accepted the light, then turned to see who it was.

His eyes went wide with surprise at the sight. "Spotted Fawn. I . . . I looked for you earlier. Didn't see you. I thought you weren't with Bad Eye's band anymore."

"I saw you, Long Arm. My heart was big, but I was afraid you would not want to see Spotted Fawn again. I went away to think. Then . . . I could not stay apart from you. I came back. Will you hate me now, Long Arm? Will you send me away?"

Longarm's brows knitted into a scowl. "Whyever would I do a thing like that, Spotted Fawn? I couldn't hate you. No matter what you've done, I couldn't ever hate you. I thought you'd know better'n that."

"I am not . . . as you remember me to be, Long Arm." The girl's eyes dropped, and he wasn't sure because of the uncertainty of the firelight and the natural duskiness of her skin, but he thought she might have been blushing as well.

"You're still the prettiest thing I ever saw on two legs, Spotted Fawn," he said. Which was damn near the truth, actually.

The girl was slim and pretty, a cascade of gleaming black hair reaching past her waist. She had a face that any artist would crave to paint, with huge, dark eyes and prominent cheekbones. Her chin was small and her lips large and sensuous. And, as Longarm remembered almighty well, soft and yielding too. She was prettier than any picture, and he said so.

"But truly, Long Arm, things have changed."

He raised an eyebrow.

"You will not hate me?" she asked.

"Never," he promised, meaning it.

Spotted Fawn reached down at her side and picked up a doeskin-wrapped bundle. He didn't know what the object was at first. Then the pretty girl—he tried to think how old she would be now; twenty? Something around that if he remembered correctly—pulled her calico blouse open and held the bundle to her breast, a little bigger and more rounded now than he'd remembered, but still shapely.

"I'll be damned," Longarm said as the front of the bundle erupted into gurgling, gulping noises. Spotted Fawn had her a kid. A tiny nit still sucking at its mama's tit.

"It is a boy child," Spotted Fawn said, pride and affection in her voice. "His small name is Rabbit. Someday he will choose a warrior's name for himself. His father is Smoking Tree. Do you remember him, Long Arm?"

"I do. Tall fellow, strong and handsome."

"Yes."

"You married Smoking Tree, did you?"

"No, Long Arm, we did not marry. We could not even though, forgive me, even though we fell much in love. Smoking Tree and I are of the same clan. When we knew that I was with child, Smoking Tree left our band. I have not seen him since that day. I will not see him ever again. But he gave me Rabbit. I will always love him. Do you hate me now that you know these things, Long Arm?"

"I told you, Spotted Fawn, I don't hate you. I couldn't. I reckon in my own way, I kinda love you too. You know?"

"Yes, Long Arm. I know. As in my way I too still love you, although I love Smoking Tree more. He knows this. I told him about you. It was only right that I do so."

Longarm nodded and puffed on his cigar, blowing smoke rings into the still night air. The pale wreaths drew a round of laughing excitement from the few children who were still awake and crowding close around to watch the grown folks at play.

Spotted Fawn nodded and stood, the boy child named Rabbit still noisily sucking at her distended nipple. "I have no man of my own, Long Arm. I sleep in a brush arbor, Rabbit and me. It is there." She pointed. "When you are ready, come to us. I will make a place for you on my pallet."

"I'll be along directly," he promised.

"Whenever you wish, Long Arm. I will wait there for you." The girl—damn, she was still young and gorgeous—stood and walked away, her posture proud and dignified even though her liaison with a clansman had shamed her among her people. She had not, he noted, tried to avoid censure by running away to another band as Smoking Tree had done. The girl had guts. But then he'd always known that about her. It was one of a great many things about her that he admired.

Besides, the pretty Ute girl was an almighty good

fuck. And that was something else that a man just plain had to admire when he came upon it.

Longarm watched her until Spotted Fawn and Rabbit disappeared into the darkness outside the circle of light created by the fire.

Then he turned his thoughts back to the business at hand.

Chapter 16

The young man giggled for no reason that Longarm could figure out. After all, he hadn't said anything particularly funny. But then Small Stones was pie-eyed, and it doesn't take much to amuse some drunks. Others might get feisty when they drank, but this fellow Small Stones was a happy drunk, laughing and friendly and full of good cheer. Full of Longarm's whiskey too, of course, which was all to the good the way Longarm saw it.

"Tell me something, my friend," Longarm said.

"We are brothers, He of the Long Arm, are we not? I will tell you anything."

"The white ranchers, Small Stones. Are your people gonna let them use the grass on your hunting lands?"

Small Stones shrugged. "That is a matter of importance, eh? It is not for me to say, my brother."

"But what does the tribe say? What do the elders say when they are in council? I know Small Stones has ears to listen when his elders speak, just as I know you are a warrior of dignity and respect. I know you would not speak out of turn, Small Stones, but I know you listen well when the old ones speak their thoughts. What do they say? Will your young men fight?"

"Fight, Arm Long? No, we have the treaty now. We are done fighting. Oh, we might fight a little . . . you know . . . if those ugly Crow come south where they do not belong or if the Shoshone try to take our horses or our women. Have you ever seen a Shoshone woman? No wonder they prefer ours, eh? Our women are beautiful. A man could not fuck a Shoshone woman unless first he covers her face with a badger's skin to make her prettier. Is this not so, my brother?"

Longarm laughed appreciatively, but was careful to avoid committing himself to an answer. After all, he'd had occasion to bed both Ute and Shoshone maidens, and had to feel a sort of divided loyalty on the subject, the full truth being that in the darkness of a smoky lodge all women look, feel, and smell pretty much the same.

"You will not fight the ranchers, you think?" he persisted, trying to get the warrior's mind back on the subject at hand.

"A white raiser of *whoa-haw* or two we might want to kill, my brother, but we do not. The soldiers would come again. Our people remember too well what happened the last time. We killed so many of you whites. The agent and the teacher and those others. But the soldiers came like a flood of blue cloth, and the booming guns. They killed too many of our people then. They were many and we were few. They would come again. That is what our elders tell us in council. Do nothing to make the soldiers come again for when they do, it is not only the warriors who die . . . our warriors are not afraid to die; you should know this. . . ."

"We know you have no fear, Small Stones. It is well known among your enemies that the Ute are a fierce and proud people who know nothing of fear."

Small Stones liked hearing that. His thin chest puffed full and he struggled against the effects of the whiskey in an attempt to sit up tall and stern and handsome while his opinion was sought by the white visitor. "We are strong, yes, but we are not many. The soldiers would come again, and our people would die. Too many. It is well, they tell us, to bide our time. We will talk, not fight. It is said by the new agent that a man of importance will be sent by the Great Father. This man will come to us. He will bring to us justice. He will tell the white raisers of cows to stay away from our treaty lands. He will make things right for us. Our elders tell us we know this to be true because the Great Father himself made to us the promise of land that will be ours alone for as long as grass grows and the waters run down from the high mountains. Is this not so, Arm Is Long?''

"It is so, Small Stones. You have the treaty. I know this to be true.''

"Yes, true. We do not need to fight. This man who comes from the Great Father will tell the other white men to go away, and they will have to leave us and our hunting lands alone for he is a man of importance. Is this not so?''

"It is so,'' Longarm said absently, his own thoughts absorbing the fact that Small Stones—and presumably the whole of the Ute Nation—did not yet know that the commissioner was dead. And if they didn't know . . . "Tell me something, Small Stones.''

"Yes, Long Arm?''

"Were there young men among you, men who want to fight as warriors once more perhaps, who would go against the advice of the elders?''

Small Stones yawned, then shrugged. "A few disagreed. You know how it is in council. Never will all agree to one thing even if the question is no more than whether it is night or day. Someone will always argue. But there was no heat in those words. We stayed, all of the people, we stayed late in our winter places, and we talked. All the people were able to speak. They listened even to me one night, yes. And I spoke, Long Arm. I said my war club has no enemy's blood on it, and I would like one time to count a coup. But . . . I admit this only because we are brothers, Arm Long . . . I was satisfied that the elders are correct. You see, I remember how it was when the soldiers came that time before. My sister died then, and my uncle. My mother, my other sisters, they would die too, I think, if the soldiers come again. No, we are done with the fighting. I will only taste battle if I am lucky enough to find a Crow or an Arapaho without friends enough to protect him. We will not fight the white man. Never again, I think. We talked much. That is why we are late coming to the grass this season. We talked many days, had much feasting.'' Small Stones giggled again. ''Not good whiskey like here, but we had meat because of the hunting on our lands where the cattle are not permitted to go. We talked many days, and it was decided. We will not fight again. We will speak with the man sent to us by the Great Father. We will ask him to stand for us when the white men want to take back our lands. We will trust the Great Father to protect his children.''

Longarm grunted. Small Stones was the sixth or seventh Ute he'd asked these questions of tonight. All of them had given him the same response. No, the Ute would not fight again over grazing rights. They would appeal to the commissioner and expect him to do what was right. The agent promised them that this would be so, and the elders agreed it was the sensible course to take. The Ute tribe would not fight, certainly not before laying their case before the special commissioner.

And no, none of them had any inkling that the man from Washington was dead.

''Tell me, Small Stones.''

''Yes, my brother?''

''What do you know about bombs and how to make them?''

''Booms, Long Arm? I do not understand. What is a boom and what does one use it for?''

"Never mind, Small Stones. Just a stray thought, that's all."

Small Stones giggled and rocked back and forth, hugging his knees to his scrawny chest and looking like he wouldn't be partying much longer. Another drink or two and he'd probably join the rest of the band in the numbed, snoring stupor that had already claimed most of them.

Longarm looked around the ring of firelight—much smaller now that the blaze had been allowed to die down—and realized that he and Small Stones seemed to be the last two still upright and mobile.

And a few seconds later Small Stones gave in to the whiskey, and Longarm found himself alone in what little was left of the night.

Longarm left his young friend lying where he was and stood, knees slightly rubbery after sitting for so long.

He stretched hugely and set off in the direction Spotted Fawn had indicated hours earlier in the evening.

He wondered if she would still be awake and waiting for him as she'd promised.

Chapter 17

The inside of the waist-high brush arbor was as dark as
a whore's soul, and Longarm could see nothing as he
dropped to hands and knees and crawled in on top of
the pine-and-blanket bed that had been made there, oc-
cupying virtually the whole of the cramped interior
space.

The tiny arbor was utilitarian, he supposed. It did
what it had to do. But it sure didn't give the room or
the comfort of a proper lodge. Nor the light, as there
was no room there for a fire to be laid.

Longarm did not have to see, however, to know that
Spotted Fawn was indeed awake. The girl's arms rose
to embrace him, drawing him down beside her with what
sounded like a glad sigh.

"Sorry, Long Arm, I was sleepy. Here, let me help."
He felt her fingers brush lightly over his shirt and down
to his trousers as she unbuttoned and unbuckled and
helped him shed his clothing. Longarm placed his Colt,
the holster wrapped in its gunbelt, at the head of the
small bed while Spotted Fawn was busy pulling off his
boots and socks. Within moments he was naked, and
once more he felt the warmth of her embrace. God, she
felt good in his arms.

It occurred to him to ask, "Where's the child?"

"With a friend. It is well, Long Arm. We are alone here, you and me."

He kissed her, Spotted Fawn's lips every bit as soft and warm and fluid as he remembered them to be. He felt the intrusion of her tongue into his mouth as she explored between his lip and gums, then dueled briefly with his own eager tongue.

"I've missed you," he said, meaning every bit of it. "I've never forgot you." And that too was mostly true, even if he thought of her seldom. A girl this lovely could not be forgotten. Not really.

He kissed her thoroughly, then pressed her down onto the soft pine boughs, his hand gently probing the vee at her crotch, fingers playing in the curly brush there. She gasped as he penetrated the veil of hair and found the already wet and receptive entry he wanted.

"Yes," the lovely girl whispered. "Yes, Long Arm."

He kissed her again, and ran his tongue down over the shelf of her jaw, across the incredible softness of her throat, and onto the hard planes of her breastbone.

He tongued her breasts, first one and then the other, and was rewarded with the faintly sweet flavor of her milk. Longarm had forgotten that Spotted Fawn was nursing. He grunted an apology, but Spotted Fawn laughed and placed her hand on the nape of his neck, pulling him tighter to her nipple and raising her chest to meet him. "Suck, Long Arm. It is good that you drink from my body." She chuckled. "Did I not drink from yours in the past? Now it is your time to drink of me."

That seemed a fair enough proposition. And yeah, this girl had swallowed his seed more than once in the past. If she wanted him now to take milk from her body, well, there was no harm in that.

He bent to her, took one distended nipple into his mouth, and gently sucked. The warm milk flowed from Spotted Fawn with a slow, sweet languor, and he allowed it to fill his mouth, savoring the taste of it for a moment before he swallowed.

"Yes, more, please, and here. Oh, yes, Long Arm my beloved, yes."

He suckled that breast for several minutes, taking the milk from her. Then Spotted Fawn laid her fingertips against his temple and urged him to the other side, where he was pleased to repeat the process.

"Do you know what this means, Long Arm?" she whispered in the darkness.

He shook his head.

"If a man takes the milk from a woman's breast it means he can never forget her. He will always love her."

Longarm grinned. "Yeah, I think I can go along with that all right, Spotted Fawn. For sure I won't ever forget you. Not that I could've anyhow." He kissed her, then let the pretty girl roll him onto his back.

"Now," she said, "it is my turn, no?"

"Now," he agreed, "it is your turn, yes." And soon he felt the cool, refreshing brush of her hair as she moved over on top of him. He felt her mouth on his nipples, sucking and pulling much as he had just done, except this time the object was not the getting of milk but the giving of pleasure.

The sensations she gave to him burned through his belly and deep into his groin. After a few minutes Spotted Fawn's tongue busily roved over his belly, dipped for a moment into his navel, and traveled further south until the soft touch of her hair fell onto his balls and he could feel the heat of her breath on his cock.

She held herself motionless there for a time, teasing him with her nearness, but withholding her touch until the anticipation drove him into a pulsing, yearning near-frenzy. He wanted her. Needed her. Now. He took hold of the back of her head and pushed, but Spotted Fawn would not let him off that easily. She went rigid, resisting his touch and making him wait long seconds more.

And then, of her own accord and in her own time, the beautiful Ute girl took him into the wet depths of her pretty mouth, the lips that were so soft and good to kiss even softer and hotter now.

She suckled him, fingertips toying with his balls and along the exquisitely sensitive shelf of flesh that separated the base of his cods from his asshole.

Spotted Fawn was good. God, she was good. She took him to dizzying heights of pleasure, and after scant minutes of that, the sensations were too much to hold back and with a groan, he burst into a long, pulsing flow that filled her mouth and nearly gagged her before she could swallow down the continuing ejaculation.

"Rest now," Spotted Fawn whispered to him. "But for a minute only, neh? When you are hard again we will come together, and I will be happy once more."

"Yes." He found her hand in the darkness and squeezed.

This, he decided, was not entirely bad.

Chapter 18

It was mid-morning and getting on toward noontime. Helluva time to be having breakfast, but then except for the young boys, who whooped and ran in circles and hunted imaginary game with their toy-sized bows and arrows, the camp hadn't shown much life to it at an ordinary get-up time. Most of the adults, certainly the male adults, appeared to be right seriously hung over. They moved around like it hurt to have to listen to all the noise of dry grass being trampled underfoot.

As for Longarm, he'd had a slightly different—and somewhat better—reason to stay abed late into the morning. Spotted Fawn, it seemed, was even more amorous and energetic in the dawn than at night. And she was one hell of a piece at night. Longarm wasn't sure, but he suspected he'd come within six or eight strokes of having his pecker wear out and fall clean off. He was that tired. But happy. Oh, yes, he surely was happy.

He lay on his back and wriggled into his clothes, then rolled over to his hands and knees to crawl backward out of the low, narrow little arbor where he'd spent such an almighty pleasant night. He spat to clear his throat, then got the morning started by lighting his first cheroot of the day. Damn, but that first one always tasted fine.

"Bad Eye," Longarm called out cheerfully, "what's for breakfast?"

The chieftain of the band winced at the sound, then managed a rather sickly smile of greeting. Judging from the way Bad Eye looked this morning, Longarm didn't know if he would still be considered a friend of the tribe, or if the Utes would look on him as the source of their head-pounding pain and banish him forever.

Fortunately, Bad Eye was in a forgiving humor. Or maybe he simply was hoping that Longarm might be able to produce some hair of the dog to help make the hurting go away. In any event, he waved for Longarm to join him at the fire.

Breakfast turned out to be a rich stew of elk chunks cooked in blood for gravy and seasoned with wild onion and some dark green stringy stuff that was either herbs put in on purpose or stray grass that got into the mixture by accident. Either way, the concoction tasted considerably better than it looked.

Longarm finished one bowl of the stew, and was hard at work on a repeat helping when some of the kids came running into camp, jabbering as fast as they could talk and gesturing off toward the north. The children reported the source of the excitement to Bad Eye, then ran off in search of their mamas or daddies or somebody else to show off to.

"What is it, Bad Eye?"

"White man and some damn Injun come." Which meant, Longarm concluded, that the damn Injun was not of the Ute people.

Longarm stood, a tin cup of sweet, scalding hot coffee held gingerly in one hand, and peered off toward the source of the excitement. Someone was coming, all right. In a large freight wagon. The people on the wagon must have wanted to make the journey mighty bad, Longarm thought, to force a rig that big and that awkward so far off the road.

The wagon was still the better part of half a mile distant, and Longarm could see for himself that there were two people riding in it. As for them being a white man and some damn Injun, well, he would withhold judgment on that subject until they came nearer.

When they did approach the camp, however, the opinion of the sharp-eyed youngsters was confirmed. They were indeed a white man and an Indian, the white man dressed like something out of a catalog offering clothing for the Great Outdoors, complete with knee-high lace-up boots with rolls of wool stockings showing at the tops, and the Indian wearing a black suit, a tidily fashioned necktie, and a derby hat.

The white man, Longarm saw, was a gent he'd seen before. Dammit.

Here in the middle of absolutely no place, one of the damned Secret Service men had gone and found him.

Longarm suspected his ass was gonna wind up in a sling now since as far as anyone back in Denver knew, Deputy Marshal Custis Long was still on assignment serving papers over in Utah.

Chapter 19

With any kind of luck, Longarm told himself, this Secret Service agent wouldn't remember him.

"Long, isn't it? Deputy Long?"

So much for luck. At least the man was smiling a nice, cheery sort of welcome. And even though he remembered who Longarm was, he would have no way of knowing what . . .

"I thought you were in Salt Lake City."

Uh, yeah. *Really* good luck he was having today. You bet.

"Yeah, well, um . . ." What the *hell* was this man's name? Was this one supposed to be Smith? Or Jones? Jeez, you would think they could've come up with something more believable than that silly combination.

"Look," the smiling—or was that smirking? Longarm couldn't tell for sure—Secret Service man said, "you don't have to tell me. I mean, I wouldn't if I was you. You know? Not really. No need anyhow. If it was my boss that was blown up, I'd be doing the exact same thing as you, Long." He shook his head and shrugged. "It doesn't make any sense to me either, taking experienced investigators who know the country and the situation around here and sending them off on a bunch of shit jobs. They could have borrowed city cops or sworn some county deputies into temporary federal service if they need to keep the routine stuff rolling, right?"

"I, um . . ."

"Oh, you don't have to say anything out loud. Not that I'd carry tales back to Denver, but you can't know that. Better for you to keep your mouth shut than trust a stranger. I won't take offense."

Surely, Longarm thought, this fella couldn't be for real. He was so . . . likable. Jeez. Nobody could be that transparent. Not really. Probably he was trying to lull Longarm into giving something away. Not that he could figure out what that something might be. But this Smith, or maybe it was Jones, he was up to some damn thing. *Had* to be.

"Excuse me a minute, would you, Long?" The man grinned and shuffled his feet some more. All right, so maybe he didn't *actually* bob his head and shuffle his feet, but that was kind of the impression he gave. Then he turned to ask the Indian with him to greet the Ute headman for him.

The Indian, it seemed, was an interpreter that the Secret Service agent had brought along with him. The Indian in the derby hat said something to Bad Eye in a guttural, slightly slurred version of the Ute tongue that even Longarm knew enough to realize wasn't an especially good rendition of the language. Fortunately, he backed up the spoken words with gestures in the pretty much universal sign language used by most all the Plains tribes, so no matter how bad he was at speaking in Ute, the two would be able to understand each other.

Bad Eye never blinked, taking it all in and responding in a fast burst of his own language.

Longarm figured if Bad Eye wanted to lay low and not let on that he spoke English, well, that was his affair. Longarm wasn't going to take the hanky off the bush and expose him.

"This man is chief of tribe," the derby Indian intoned in a sonorous voice, not necessarily accurately, but spoken with conviction regardless. "His name is Dead Sea. He welcome Agent Smit as his white father." Which at least solved that small puzzle. This was the one who called himself Smith.

"Tell Dead Sea . . . ," Smith began, and the dance had begun. Longarm figured this was apt to go on for quite a while, and judging by the preliminary rounds, would likely end up with all parties hopelessly confused.

Hell, there were worse things that could happen.

"Excuse me, Smith," Longarm said in a soft voice while the two Indians were busy grunting at each other.

"Yes, Long?"

"I reckon you got things under control here, so I think I'll move along. No sense in the two of us duplicating efforts, right?"

"Certainly, Long." The so-called Smith smiled a smile that Longarm would have sworn looked genuine . . . if he didn't already know better than to trust the son of a bitch. "And don't worry. I won't say a word to anyone back in Denver about . . . you know."

"Right. Thanks."

The two shook hands, and Longarm placed himself behind Smith's Indian where Bad Eye could see him, then sketched a few signs in the air to tell Bad Eye goodbye, that they would talk more later.

Bad Eye grunted loudly and made signs to say thanks for the whiskey. Which confused the hell out of the derby Indian, and brought Smith into the picture as he hurried to explain that they had a wagon load of stuff as presents for the great Ute people but that they hadn't brought whiskey with them because that would have been against the law.

Longarm hid his amusement and got the hell out of there while he could manage to do so without laughing out loud. He was pretty sure Bad Eye wouldn't explain what he'd meant by the sign. And if he did, the interpreter would likely get the explanation wrong anyway. Longarm suspected Smith wasn't going to learn a whole hell of a lot while he was there. But bless the handsome young fellow's heart for trying, right?

Longarm got his gear together and headed north, toward Florissant and the quick route back to civilization.

Chapter 20

Longarm was seated in a rocking chair on the front porch when Henry got home from work. It was well past dark already, but Longarm was content enough. His belly was full and he had a cheroot twined in his fingers. It was not entirely unknown for the dedicated clerk to work long hours whenever necessary, and Longarm was willing to wait however long it took so he could be caught up on whatever might have taken place while he'd been away.

"Hello, Longarm. Come inside away from the mosquitoes," Henry suggested as he unlocked his front door and led the way in.

Longarm hadn't particularly noticed any mosquitoes around, but then maybe the smoke from his cigar kept them away. He stood, yawning, and followed his friend indoors. "Hope you don't mind me waiting for you here," he said.

"It's the sensible thing to do." Henry smiled and continued with the task of lighting the lamps in his parlor, then moving back into the kitchen with Longarm trailing close behind. "You can't exactly show yourself at the office right now, can you."

"No, but I'm sure anxious to hear what the other boys

are findin'. Me, I didn't learn much so far. Except that I'd swear the Utes I talked with didn't do the bombing themselves an' don't know anything about anybody else with such a plan either.''

''I wish I could give you a better-informed report than I have, Longarm, but you're the first of our renegades—if I can use that term—who has gotten back to the city. I did get a brief wire from Dutch. He is at the Ute agency headquarters over on the west slope. He says he has found nothing so far, but will continue his inquiries there. Smiley is in Canon City. God knows what he is working on down there. Talking with some of his less reputable friends inside the prison possibly. But that is mere guesswork. All I know about it is where he went. He did not tell me why. As for the rest of our people''— Henry shrugged—''they are scattered hither and yon but have not yet reported back anything worth knowing.''

''And the official investigation?'' Longarm asked.

Henry's expression turned sour. ''It is a muddle, Long. A complete mess. The acting U.S. attorney has people dashing around in a dozen directions at once, so many of them they stumble over each other and get in each other's way, but no one has come up with anything worth knowing. Which is hardly surprising under the circumstances.''

''I still don't understand. . . .''

''Let's not get into that, all right?'' Henry pleaded. He opened the firebox door on his range and added wood to a low-burning fire there, then lifted the lid of a pot left warm on the stove surface. A beefy aroma rose enticingly to fill the room.

''Damn, that smells good,'' Longarm said.

''My housekeeper,'' Henry explained. ''She is a better-than-average cook. There is more than enough for two.''

''I wasn't dropping hints. Honest. I ate on my way over here from the train station.''

"Even so. . . ."

Longarm shook his head, but so as not to be impolite said, "Is that coffee I see there? I'd take some of that if you was to offer."

"Give it a minute for the fire to build up. It will be hot soon."

Longarm nodded and helped himself to a seat at the table, while Henry dished up a bowl of rich, chunky stew for himself and took a tin plate of crusty rolls out of the warming oven. "Are you sure you won't join me?"

"No, thanks."

Henry began eating, but gave his attention to the report Longarm presented, such as it was, on what little he'd learned down south. Halfway through Henry excused himself to fetch coffee for both of them, then once again concentrated on listening.

"An' that's about it," Longarm concluded. About the only thing he had neglected to mention was the time he'd spent with Spotted Fawn. That was none of the government's business, nor Henry's either.

Henry nodded. "You say this fellow Smith recognized you?"

"He damn sure did. Even remembered the assignment I was given. He's sharper than I thought. Don't underestimate him. Nor Jones either, I suppose. The two of 'em seem to run in a pack, an' I'd guess one is likely as good as the other. Which is a sight better'n I gave them credit for to begin with."

Henry sighed. "I suppose that is why the acting U.S. attorney decided to rely on them to run the investigation instead of using our own people."

"Even if it did make sense, dammit, I'd still resent it. Billy was *our* boss and *our* friend. These Washington boys are total strangers that never even met him. We got the right, Henry. God knows we got the right to be in on the hunt for his killers."

"I am sure the acting U.S. attorney is doing what he genuinely thinks is best."

"Bullshit. You don't think no such thing. You think just like the rest of us. That Cotton is playing politics with this investigation. Wantin' to make himself look good to the attorney general back in Washington City. That's why he put Smith an' Jones in charge. He wants them to give him high marks when they get back home, never mind what they do or don't find out here. Cotton wants the U.S. attorney's job permanently. Finding Billy's murderer is secondary now that there's a vacancy that needs filling."

"I have every confidence in the acting U.S. attorney and his motives," Henry declared, perhaps a trifle too firmly for credibility.

Longarm just grinned at him and said, "Bullshit."

"I beg your pardon?"

"Henry, you're transparent as a pane of glass. You can't abide the son of a bitch. I bet if you had to shake hands with the man, you'd run right away an' wash yourself just as quick as he was outa sight."

"Whyever would you say—?"

"Because," Longarm replied, cutting him off, "you can't hardly bring yourself to call the man by name. It's 'acting U.S. attorney' this and 'acting U.S. attorney' that. I don't think you've once called the man by name, always by title. The whole damn mouthful. Is he really that bad, Henry?"

Henry looked like he wanted to deny the obvious, but after a moment he capitulated with a slump of his shoulders and a sad frown. "He is a complete prick, Longarm. And of course you are right. I can scarcely stand to be in the same room with him. To think that I have to take orders from him now after working so many years with a fine man like Marshal Vail."

"You could resign," Longarm suggested.

Henry gave him a scathing look. "Not until the killer

or killers are brought to justice. Not one second before that time, I swear it. I owe Marshal Vail that much.''

"Yeah,'' Longarm said, draining the last of his coffee and pushing back away from the table. "You an' me both.''

"What will you do next, Longarm?''

"Talk to the driver an' footman that was on the coach that day. Maybe one of them will have seen something useful. They did survive, didn't they, the both of 'em?''

"Yes.''

"You wouldn't have their names, would you?''

"At the office. Not here. And no, I don't happen to remember them off the top of my head.'' Henry pursed his lips in concentration for a moment, then said, "It wouldn't do for you to be seen in the Federal Building. After all, you are officially in Utah right now, and we don't want the acting U.S. attorney to know his instructions are not being, shall we say, adhered to with full confidence. He has quite a temper, and if he started looking into the whereabouts of all our people, he might find a rather large number of surprises. Worse, we might find ourselves cut off from any opportunity to conduct the investigation the way we think it should be done.

"What I want you to do, Long, is to meet me tomorrow morning. At that cafe on Colfax . . . Maxwell's, is it?''

Longarm remembered the place. He'd had coffee there often enough before. "What time?''

"Would nine be convenient? I could step out for coffee and a doughnut about then. And bring the pertinent information about the people on the carriage with me.''

"Convenient, Henry? I'd find it convenient to walk through fire if it'd help put Billy's killers behind bars. Or better yet put the sons of bitches underground. Nine o'clock at Maxwell's. I'll be there.''

Longarm did not bother reminding Henry that the unauthorized disclosure of case records would be a violation of federal law. He knew Henry wouldn't care about that any more than Longarm did.

He said his good-byes and left Henry alone with an almighty tasty-looking peach cobbler that the housekeeper had also left in the warming oven. For a bachelor, old Henry had himself set up pretty comfortably, Longarm thought as he retrieved his hat and headed out into the night air.

Chapter 21

It was just damn near depressing, thinking about the contrast between the way Henry had his life arranged and Longarm's own, much more spartan existence in the boardinghouse over on the other side of Cherry Creek. Not that he was uncomfortable in the small room he'd occupied for so many years now. Not that he was jealous of Henry either. Truly he wasn't. But, well, all of a sudden the evening that loomed before him looked kinda . . . empty. Lonesome, almost. And dammit, he didn't feel like going out drinking and playing cards with a bunch of strangers. Not tonight, he didn't.

Instead he wandered the streets for a bit, smoking and pondering, not really wanting to go back to an empty room and a cold bed, and after a time he decided he might as well drop by to see, on the off chance sort of, if Deborah happened to be home and, well, not doing anything right at the moment. Just in case.

That decision accomplished, he commenced to feeling considerably better. And it wasn't like he was taking time away from the investigation. There wasn't anything he could do now until he got those names from Henry come tomorrow morning. Right? Damn right.

Satisfied, Longarm tossed the stub of his cheroot into

the gutter and stalked off in search of a passing hack he could flag down and get to take him to Deborah's place.

"Custis!" She sounded surprised. And kinda mad too, he thought. She said his name like she was reporting the presence of dog shit on the bottom of her shoe.

"Didn't you get my note?"

"What note?"

"I sent you a letter. A couple days ago."

"You sent me a letter a couple days ago? Last week you stood me up. I thought we were going to have a long weekend together. Did that slip your mind, Custis?"

"Dammit, Debbie, be fair. My boss was murdered. I'm sure you heard 'bout that. All of us been busy as a kicked-over nest of ants, running around trying to figure out who done it. I had to go down south in the mountains. Didn't have time to plan for it nor to come by an' tell you what was up. But I sent you that letter from down there. I swear I did."

"I haven't seen any letter."

"It's only been a couple days, I told you. It'll show up in another day or two."

She sniffed haughtily. But he thought she looked a little less angry. Maybe. He hoped.

This one, this woman in front of him, well, Deborah was kinda special. That's all there was to it.

Not that she was all that much to look at. At least not the first few times you looked at her. She was a big gal. Big all over, from the bones out. Tall, with wide hips and big tits, and likely she weighed almost as much as Longarm did. But then she was damn near as tall as he was too, and her weight was distributed in a mighty fetching series of curves and indentations.

She had high cheekbones, big lips that he happened already to know were plenty soft and mobile, big furry caterpillars of eyebrows over huge brown eyes, and a kinky-curly mass of strawberry-blond hair that no amount of brushing could ever quite tame. She was Irish and looked it, with her pale, lightly freckled complexion and strong jawline.

She was strong too, with arms that could pick up most patients to turn them over or wash them or whatever, and legs that, although shapely, were powerful enough to bust ribs if she ever decided to clamp down on a man in, say, a fit of passion or something.

She was . . . hell, she was fine. That's all there was to it. She was fine.

And if she didn't seem especially beautiful at the first or third or maybe tenth inspection, eventually a man had to ask himself why he was spending all that time staring at her, and when he did that he just naturally had to come to the conclusion that this big old Irish gal had something special about her. An air, an aura, something that happened to those close by when she was around.

Rooms seemed to open up and get brighter when Deborah walked into them. Colors became clearer and images sharper. Sounds were lighter and happier when she was nearby, and there was always joy and laughter trailing in her wake wherever she walked.

Longarm damn sure liked this handsome woman in her primly starched white dress and bird-shaped nurse's cap. He hoped he hadn't gone and alienated her. He removed his Stetson and held it before him in both hands, kind of giving the idea that he was wringing the brim, but at the same time being careful not to muss the felt. After all, it was a good hat and he didn't want to ruin it while he was making like Little Boy Lost.

He kept his eyes down, a contrite expression on his face and a load of very genuine hope in his heart. "I didn't go to make you mad," he said. "I'm sorry that I stood you up. You did hear about Billy, didn't you?"

She gave him a strange look that he couldn't quite interpret. Then, after a time that seemed uncomfortably long to him, she sighed and stepped back out of the doorway, pushing the screen door open so he could come inside. "You really mailed me a letter?"

He nodded. "From a place called Florissant. You'll see. Surely it'll turn up in a day or two."

"All right then. I expect I can forgive you. For a day or two anyway. But that letter had better be on the way, with the right postmark and date on it and everything, Custis, or I'll be so mad you'll wish you never came back."

Longarm grinned. And stepped inside Deborah's foyer.

He managed to wait until the door was closed behind him and none of the neighbors might see. Then he took the gal—the whole wonderful armful of her—into his embrace and kissed her with all the intensity of a drowning man getting a breath of air.

Lordy, but he'd missed her. More even than he'd realized.

Chapter 22

"No, now let go of me for a minute, Custis. I have to get out of this uniform."

"That's pretty much what I had in mind too," he confessed with a wink and a wicked leer.

Deborah laughed. And gave him a love tap on the head that damn near buckled his knees. He hated to think what it would feel like if she ever whacked him while she was pissed off. Likely it would knock him clean off his feet and send him ass-over-teacup rolling into the next room. All in all, he decided, it was a supposition he would rather not test in actual fact.

"Not before I have my bath, Custis. You know that."

He nodded. Deborah was nothing if not clean. She was fanatical about it. Probably it had something to do with her training as a nurse, he suspected, but the first thing she always insisted on when she came away from work was getting herself scrubbed clean. And not just a spit-and-dab job of it either. She had to have herself a proper tub bath, and there wouldn't be any peace to be found here if he tried to distract her or cozy her out of it. This was a gal who knew how to satisfy a man—which he was pretty sure had nothing at all to do with being a nurse, but a lot with being one hell of a woman—but she wouldn't allow a finger on her, hardly, until she'd taken her bath.

"Do you need some help?"

"You can draw some water for me. It should be hot by now."

Longarm went off to find the bucket while Deborah wrestled the slipper-shaped copper tub out of the kitchen pantry where she stored it during the day.

She didn't need any help dragging it out onto the floor, heavy though it was, while he filled the bucket with water from the reservoir built onto the side of the wood box on the kitchen range. At least Longarm supposed it was still called that, even though Deborah burned coal in her stove. That was a question that had never occurred to him before. Anyway, he carried water to the tub until the reservoir was empty, then used the small pump built conveniently right onto the kitchen sink to draw more water, first to refill the hot water reservoir so it would be ready for the next time, then to add cold water to the tub until Deborah told him the temperature of the bathwater was to her liking.

"There's room enough for two," she suggested.

Longarm took a skeptical look at the narrow tub.

"Trust me," she said, a somewhat impish look about her.

"If you put it that way . . ."

Deborah shed her uniform, its starch long since wilted and some unpleasantly red stains marring the white cloth after a day at the hospital, and Longarm hastened to shuck out of his clothes.

My, but this one was all woman. Proud of it too. There was no false modesty about her. She knew she looked good, and she made no attempt to hide herself from the admiration that was her proper due . . . and which he was pleased to give to her.

Her tits were big, but they barely sagged. Eventually they would, he supposed, but that time was still some years away. She had large, pale nipples and a dense thatch of reddish-blond hair at her crotch. Her belly was flat and her thighs smooth and pretty despite the heavy muscling that lay barely seen beneath the surface of her unblemished skin. She had delicate ankles and feet that seemed too small to carry her.

All in all, Longarm thought, she presented one dandy figure.

"Do you like?" she challenged, turning and preening and showing off for his pleasure.

"Plenty," he admitted.

"You're just buttering me up, aren't you?"

"You want to use butter tonight?" he asked with a grin. "If that's what you want . . ."

Deborah laughed, then stepped into the tub. She settled breast-deep into the hot water and closed her eyes for a moment, then opened them again and said, "You can scrub my back if you really want to."

"It'd be a pleasure, ma'am."

"Oh, my. How formal."

"Whatever the lady wishes," Longarm said, trying to sound detached and proper about it.

He fetched a dish of soap off the counter near the sink and scooped a couple of fingers of it into his palm, then stepped over behind Deborah and began washing her. He washed her back. And continued on around to the front. Her breasts were full and heavy, slick and slippery with the combination of water and soap. He gently lathered them, giving special attention to her nipples, which by now were as hard and erect as Longarm's stiff pecker.

"I thought I said something about washing my back," Deborah declared.

"I can quit if you'd like."

"Don't you dare."

He continued washing her, and Deborah closed her eyes and gave herself over to the sensations.

93

"Stand up," he said. "I can't wash what's underwater, y'know."

She nodded, and he took her hand to steady her as she stood in the tub. Lordy, but she was gorgeous standing there all wet, her skin gleaming in the lamplight. She looked like a Grecian statue. But prettier.

Longarm took his time. Genuinely washing her, true, but also damn well enjoying the feel of her body under his hands. He washed everything in reach. And reached everything possible.

"My goodness. That feels nice."

"Better'n when you do it your own self?" he teased.

"Mmm. Better. Oh, do that again, Custis. Yes, there. I don't think I've ever . . . *oh*!" She jumped a little, rising onto tiptoes as his wet, soapy fingers probed between the nicely round cheeks of Deborah's ass.

"Careful. We wouldn't want you fallin' down and breaking something. Not yet."

"I take that to mean it would be all right if I were to break something later?"

"Let's just say that if you're gonna do something like that, let's at least get the timing right. I happen to be so horny right now I could honk."

She laughed, and Longarm gave her his best imitation of a goose's honk by way of demonstration, causing her to laugh all the louder.

"All right, Custis. Let me rinse off now. Then it's your turn."

"You really think we can both of us fit into that little thing?"

"Trust me," she repeated with a knowing smile.

And damned if she wasn't right about that. They did fit. Of course, in order to accomplish that feat, selected parts of his anatomy had to be tucked inside certain portions of hers. Just to keep them out of the way, so to speak, so that things didn't get bent or broken.

It was a sacrifice, but what the hell. He made it, accepting the necessity with manly fortitude.

This was, he decided afterward, without question the most enjoyable bath he could remember taking in just ever so long.

Chapter 23

Longarm was content. Drained and worn down to a limp and aching nub, but content despite that. There was a hollow void down where his balls used to be—were they still there? he wasn't sure—and a sense of lassitude that kept tugging him deeper and deeper into the soft clouds of sleep. He couldn't be certain, but he thought he could hear himself snore just a bit every now and then.

Deborah stirred at his side. They had adjourned to her bedroom a couple of hours earlier, leaving the tub where it was. She'd said she would empty and clean it in the morning, that at the moment there were more interesting things to do.

And he'd had to agree with that assessment. Indeed there had been.

Now he was drowsy and content, the weight of her tight against his side and her breath warm and moist on the side of his throat. He liked having her there. Liked everything about her. Was glad he'd had the good sense to come there tonight.

"Are you awake, Custis?" she whispered.

"Mmm."

"It's all right, you know. You don't have to pretend with me."

"Pretend what?"

"About . . . you know. The killings."

He sighed and considered opening his eyes, then thought better of it. He kind of wished Deborah would shut up now. He was sleepy. But he didn't want to offend her. He just wished he knew what the hell she was talking about.

"Killings?"

"You know. The bomb."

"Oh, yeah. That."

"It's just that you don't have to pretend when we're alone, Custis. Really. I already know."

"Know? Know what, honey?"

"About the marshal. Your boss."

"Mmm." Billy. God, he missed Billy Vail. There never was a better boss than him.

"I know you have to keep up appearances when you're in public, Custis, but I already know. I mean, I'm not supposed to know. I don't think any of the other nurses do. But I met the marshal once. Do you remember? We were having dinner and the marshal and his wife came in. You introduced them to me that evening. Do you recall?"

He didn't, but he supposed that did not matter now. He just wished Deborah would let him sleep. Then come morning he would meet Henry and get back to the business of finding out who the son of a bitch was that had murdered Billy.

And the others too, of course. He didn't mean that their deaths weren't just as important. But it was Billy's murder that hurt the worst, the one he and the rest of the boys wanted so bad to avenge.

"Is that why you haven't visited, Custis? Is it because you were afraid I would put two and two together and say something? I wouldn't. Honestly. You can trust me."

He remembered her saying something about trusting

her before, and she'd sure been right about that. The two of them fit into that tub just nice as nice could be. She . . .

"Visit who, honey? You? I already told you. I woulda been by to see you but I was down south in the mountains. Had to talk to some Indians, see if one of them might've made that bomb and thrown it."

"Not me, Custis. The marshal."

"What about the marshal?" he mumbled, his mind unfocused as he rode on the thin edge that divided sleep from wakefulness.

"Is that why you haven't been to see him? You don't have to worry, dear. I won't give it away."

"See who, dammit?"

"Custis! Are you paying attention to me at all? I said is that why you haven't been by to visit with Marshal Vail?"

Longarm felt a jolt go through him as sharp and piercing as a bolt of lightning.

He jerked upright, startling Deborah and sending her tumbling half off the narrow bed that really was intended for one person to sleep in.

"Did you ask whyn't I *visit Billy Vail,* girl?"

Chapter 24

It was almost four in the morning by the time Longarm made it to the hospital. He would have been willing to run all the way from Deborah's house if he had to, but in fact he'd been able to locate a hackney with its driver sleeping inside and the horses hipshot and dozing. The hack dropped him at the back of the hospital and rolled silently away into the night, leaving Longarm shivering in the predawn air.

The back door was unlocked, as Deborah had told him it would be. Inside, the hospital was silent and dark save for lamps burning at the empty nursing stations on each floor. Longarm had no idea where the overnight nurses had disappeared to at this hour. Wherever they were, they were paying no attention to the sleeping patients.

Longarm's boots rang hollow and haunting on the polished hardwood floor of the main corridor. He climbed a service stairwell—again relying on Deborah's detailed instructions—and barely cracked the fire door open to look down the third-floor hallway.

As he'd been told to expect, there was a guard sitting outside the last door on the right. Unfortunately the guard—a man Longarm did not know and was pretty sure he'd never seen before—was wide awake. Longarm had been more than halfway hoping the guard would have imitated the nurses and disappeared into the linen storage areas or laundry rooms or whatever to nap until the commencement of activities come daylight.

Muttering under his breath, Longarm retraced his steps back down the stairs, getting well away from any likelihood of chance discovery while he took time to think this through. He didn't want to bull his way forward right now and risk fucking up. Not while he had no idea just what was going on here, he didn't.

Longarm mulled over the possibilities. Then he poked around in several of the rooms that were posted with signs warning away all but officially authorized personnel, doctors and the like.

Ten minutes later he climbed the stairs again, this time going up the central stairway and making no effort to muffle the sounds of his footsteps.

When he appeared on the third-floor landing, he did not look quite the same as when he'd arrived. His broad-brimmed Stetson hat was missing, and his hair was slightly unkempt, as if he'd been roused from sleep and hadn't taken time to comb it as yet.

A slightly soiled white smock had replaced his usual tweed coat. It hung open at the front, exposing his shirt-front, vest, and necktie. Now there was no gunbelt or holster at his waist. Instead he wore one of those chest-listening devices draped around his neck. Stethoscope, was that it? He was having a mite of trouble remembering the name of the gadget. There was sort of a metal headband clamped around his head with a magnifying glass attached to it. The thing—he had no earthly idea of the proper name for it—was uncomfortable as hell to wear. But, he hoped, impressive to look at. Which was all he wanted it for anyway.

He had a fistful of pencils in the breast pocket of his smock, and was carrying a handful of papers that he'd purloined at random from a deserted nursing station downstairs. He hoped they were not crucially important to anyone because he might or might not have a chance to return them later.

Walking slowly and perusing the paperwork while he did so—not that the notes he found there told him anything; they might as well have been in a different language for all he could figure them out—he entered a room about halfway down the third-floor hall.

An elderly man was asleep on a bed there, his toothless mouth hanging open and a rasping series of loud snores streaming out of him. The old fellow looked barely alive, but the snoring at least proved that he would likely make it through this night anyway.

Longarm stood by the doorway for several minutes, wishing he could light a cheroot while he waited. After he thought sufficient time had passed, he went back into the hallway, his boots loud on the bare floor. The guard down at the far end of the hall pretty much had to notice him. Hell, he was the only thing moving in the whole damn hospital, or anyway so it seemed.

Longarm ostentatiously pulled his Ingersoll watch from his vest pocket and inspected it—it was 4:38 A.M.—then faked a yawn and sauntered down in the direction of the room with the guard outside it.

"Good morning," he said.

"Good morning, Doctor."

"Excuse me, please. I suppose I should go ahead and check on Mr. Janus while I'm here. Save myself a second trip later this morning." Janus was the name Deborah told him they were using for the "patient" in 342.

"Yes, sir," the guard said. "Uh, Doctor? Could I ask you a favor, please?"

Longarm's heart skipped a beat, and a frog the size of a jackrabbit leaped into the back of his throat. What if this guy had a medical question? Jesus!

Well, if he did there was only one thing to do. Lie.

Stand there and lie like a sonuvabitch and hope the man wouldn't know any better.

"Certainly," he said, trying to sound bored and unconcerned, but not sure he pulled it off too well. Whether he did or not, the guard didn't seem to notice. And that was what counted.

"Will you be inside there a few minutes?"

"Probably. Is there something you need?"

"Yes, sir. I got to take a crap, Doctor, but I'm not supposed to leave this door. If you wouldn't mind . . ."

Longarm smiled. Didn't have to fake it either. "Go ahead. I'll stay with him until you get back."

"Thanks, Doc. I mean . . . Doctor. Thanks an awful lot." The guard—he looked young enough to barely be shaving—looked embarrassed and eager and grateful all at the same time. He stood, bobbing his head, and hurried off down the hall toward the main staircase that Longarm had come up just a few minutes earlier.

Longarm waited until the guard reached the stairs and was on his way down.

Then he shoved the room door open and went inside to see the patient listed on hospital records as Arthur James Janus.

Chapter 25

"It's about time you showed up."

"My God. It's really you." Longarm felt . . . he didn't know what exactly. Relieved. Pleased. Just about overflowing with whatever else might have been mixed into that stew of abraded nerves and uncertain feelings.

"Of course it's me," Billy Vail said, sounding more peeved than anything. "Who the hell were you expecting?"

"I didn't . . . dammit, Billy, they said you were dead."

"Dead? Don't be absurd. You can see perfectly well that I'm just fine."

"Yeah, but . . ."

Billy's normally pink complexion paled. "Someone told you I was killed? But they told me you, all of you, were in on the secret."

"Secret, Boss? The only secret I know about is the one that kept anybody from knowing you're still alive. They said you were dead. And the commissioner an' his wife an' the U.S. attorney too. They said all of you were killed by that bomb blast."

"I'm fine. As you can see for yourself. So are Jason Terrell and Commissioner Troutman."

"The U.S. attorney is alive too? And the commissioner? But they said. . . ." Longarm shut up. And frowned. What the hell was going on here anyway?

"They're fine, Longarm. We three survived the bombing."

"You've seen them your own self? Talked to them?"

"No, I haven't left this room since they put me here. But I was told . . . oh. I see what you mean. It could be that Jason and the commissioner are dead too, I suppose. But what reason would anyone have for lying about this? About any of it?"

"Billy, I'll be damned if I know. Yet. But it does make for kind of an interesting question, doesn't it?"

"Doesn't it just," Billy Vail agreed.

"They," Longarm said. "Just who might 'they' be?"

"The assistant United States attorney for one. Cotton, his name is."

"Uh-huh. Except he's acting U.S. attorney now that Mr. Terrell is s'posed to be dead. Along with you."

"Let me see. Who else?" Billy mused. "I've spoken with the majority leader of the state senate, Senator Goodwin. And Congressman Forsythe, of course. He's been by to see me several times. Mostly, though, it has been J. B. who has been in to see how I am. He brings me magazines, some wines that the hospital people won't allow, little favors like that. He has been very thoughtful really. He brings me news too." Billy scowled. "Like what you and the others have been doing as part of the investigation."

"Now ain't that interesting," Longarm said, "because me and all the regular fellows been sent off on shit details while the investigation into the bombing has been taken over by a couple gents named Smith and Jones from the Secret Service."

"That isn't at all what J. B. has been telling me."

"Billy, like I said before, dammit, what we've all been told is that you, all of you, were dead. Wiped out.

They even had a burial service for you. Dandy eulogy, coffins, all that.''

"What about my wife, Longarm? Surely she has been told the truth. They said she was told. They said she knew not to worry.''

"I wouldn't know 'bout that, Billy. I saw Henry last night. He said your widow—I mean your wife—was torn up pretty bad by the news you were dead. She was at the funeral, of course. If she knew the truth, then she's one hell of a fine actress, for she surely looked like a grieving widow that day. After the funeral, Henry told me, she went back East to stay with her sister or somebody for a spell.''

"Damn,'' Billy grumbled.

"Billy, how the hell did you live through that mess anyhow? I was there that day. It was a helluva explosion. I saw for myself when the ambulance people picked you up an' carried you off. You were drenched all over with blood. I remember that clear as if I could still see it. For that matter, I still can whenever I close my eyes, though I try not to.''

"That wasn't my blood, Longarm. It was Mrs. Troutman's. She took nearly all the force of the blast.''

Longarm raised an eyebrow and waited for Billy to explain.

"We were all inside by then, if you recall. Commissioner Troutman was in a fine mood. Laughing, pleased, eager to get started on his assignment. His wife saw someone in the crowd that she thought she recognized. She leaned forward to wave to whoever it was, and that was when the bomb was thrown in through the side window.''

"Yeah, I remember that much.''

"The fuse was short. There was no time for any of us to do anything. The bomb fell onto the floor at the back of the carriage and rolled under Mrs. Troutman's skirts.''

"Jesus," Longarm muttered.

"Really. It was ugly, I can tell you that. She was torn up pretty badly, or so I was told later. Not that I can personally attest to it, but I can certainly believe it. They said she took nearly all the blast." Billy frowned again, obviously thinking that "they" had had much to say. And not all of it was necessarily true.

"But you, Boss, how'd you and the others survive?"

"Like I told you, Mrs. Troutman took most of the force of the explosion. They said the commissioner was badly injured but that he will recover. I was knocked out by the concussion of the blast, and I would assume the others were too. When I came to again I was down-stairs in this hospital. I was covered in dried blood and had a headache. My ears were ringing, and for a couple days there I couldn't hear very well, but that was about the extent of my injuries. There was no permanent harm done."

"Did they say anything about the commissioner's leg, Billy?"

"No. Why?"

"Because it was blown clean off, that's why. I saw that myself. Saw one of the ambulance attendants pick it up an' lay it on the stretcher they'd put his body on. An' I woulda sworn, Billy, that the commissioner was already dead at that point, even though, of course, I didn't walk right up an' look at him. He just . . . had that empty, used-up look. You know what I mean."

The U.S. marshal nodded. He too had seen more than his fair share of dead men.

Longarm grunted. "How'd they talk you into playing dead, Billy?"

"They said the bomb was thrown by a faction of ren-egade Ute Indians who were afraid the commissioner was going to rule against them in his recommendations to the president and Congress. They said the president himself asked that the public be told we all were dead so the renegades would think they succeeded and not make another attempt, perhaps a more successful one this time, to assassinate the special commissioner. They said the president asked for our cooperation with this to give Commissioner Troutman time to complete his assignment.''

''That's what 'they' said, is it?'' Longarm asked.

Billy nodded.

''Boss, I think you and me and the rest of the boys need to be doing some real serious work here. There's stuff going on that I can't begin to figure out. But I damn sure intend to find out what it is.''

Chapter 26

"Doctor? Excuse me, Doctor. I just wanted you to know that I'm back on duty now. You can leave any time you want." The guard smiled and ducked back out of the room.

Longarm, perched on the side of Billy's hospital bed with a cheroot between his teeth, did not want to take any chances on the guard overhearing something he shouldn't. Smooth as glass he shifted from being a deputy into his assumed identity as a doctor. "Well, Mr. Janus, I'll leave you now. You seem to be doing just fine, however. There is nothing for you to worry about." Longarm gave Billy a long, level look and repeated, "Nothing. Do you understand?"

"I do, Doctor. Thank you."

Longarm stood, and the two rather formally shook hands, even though the door was closed between them and the guard outside. "I'll stop by again real soon," Doctor Long promised.

"I look forward to seeing you again." Billy sounded like he meant that too. And no wonder, Longarm thought. Now that he knew the game wasn't what it seemed to be, it would be mighty difficult for Billy to stay cooped up there like a sheep in the slaughterhouse.

Which might well be an unpleasantly apt simile.

It had occurred to Longarm by now—and almost certainly must have crossed Billy's mind too, or damned soon would—that whoever was behind this charade could not possibly hope to get away with it forever.

And it just could be that eventually "they"—whoever *they* were—would conclude that long-term secrecy demanded the elimination of anyone who would be in a position to dispute all the false claims that were so casually being thrown around.

It just could be that eventually Billy Vail, U.S. Attorney Terrell, and Commissioner Troutman would have to be eliminated in order to assure their silence.

Thinking about that, Longarm glanced quickly over his shoulder to assure himself that the door remained shut, then tugged at his watch chain. A sharp jerk broke the fragile link that had been soldered onto the butt of his hideout gun, freeing the .44 derringer from the chain. Without needing to explain, Longarm passed the little gun—as nasty in its bite as it was small in the hand—to Billy, and handed over as well the half-dozen loose rimfire cartridges that he had put in a pocket of the smock.

Not that Billy would necessarily need a firearm here in Denver's finest hospital.

But a man never knew. Especially when neither of them had any idea what this shit was all about.

Billy tucked the derringer out of sight beneath the covers and nodded a silent thank-you.

"Good-bye, Mr. Janus."

"Good-bye, Doctor."

The guard was effusive in his thanks for the "doctor" who'd stood in for him with the patient. Without thinking about it, Longarm tried to touch the brim of his Stetson by way of acknowledgment, then realized a trifle too late that what he was wearing was not the familiar hat but the gadget with the magnifying glass attached.

He covered the lapse by scratching his head, then muttered an absentminded good-bye to the guard before turning and ambling down the long, empty corridor, his attention appearing to center on the sheaf of papers he still carried.

In fact his attention was focused on the hospital's hallways, or what he could see of them.

He was pretty sure there were no other guards posted anywhere on the third floor, but he had no way to determine if any might be found elsewhere.

Other doors under guard would tend to point to the presence, and therefore the survival, of Attorney Terrell and Commissioner Troutman, while the absence of any other guards in the hospital would hint of an opposite conclusion.

That was something he would have to ask Deborah about, Longarm thought.

He had spent enough time with Billy that people were starting to show up for work now, and he could hear voices and footsteps from the lower floors. At the third-floor nursing station there was actually a nurse visibly on duty now, although the area had been empty when he came upstairs. Apparently these hospital people were fairly early to get on the job. All the better, he supposed, to wake patients out of their sleep so annoying procedures could be followed and unnecessary fees imposed.

In any event, Longarm did not want to risk exposure as a phony wandering through the place. If he were found out, it would call attention to the visit in Billy's room and alert whoever it was who was behind this craziness. Almost as bad, it would keep him from repeating the performance. Better, he decided, to be cautious until he had something of a handle on what was going on. Accordingly he did not try to investigate the rest of the hospital corridors, but settled for brief glances down the main hallways as he passed the second-floor landing and got back down to the ground floor, where he quickly returned his doctor disguise to the laundry room where he'd found the smock.

He had to admit that he felt a helluva lot better when he once again had the familiar weight of a .44 Colt strapped at his waist. For a little while there he'd felt purely naked, walking around completely unarmed like he'd been.

A check of the Ingersoll showed that he still had time enough to stop by the boardinghouse for a shave and a change of clothes before he would have to leave for his meeting with Henry.

And wouldn't Henry be pleased when he learned Billy Vail was still alive. Lordy, he reckoned.

Come to think of it, Longarm realized, he probably should get Henry off by himself somewhere before he delivered that news. Otherwise the coffee-and-crullers crowd at Maxwell's Cafe might overhear some whooping and hollering that would draw unwelcome attention.

Chapter 27

Henry's reaction was even more than Longarm had expected it would be. After an initial yelp of joy, the prim and proper clerk dropped to his knees, good suit pants and all, clasped his hands, and began whispering. Right there on Colfax Avenue in front of God and everybody.

But then, Longarm realized, that was the whole idea, wasn't it? Longarm wasn't a praying man himself. But he could sure understand it in this case. News as good as this didn't come along just every day of the week.

"He's alive, Long? Billy is really alive? You've seen him? Talked to him?"

Longarm affirmed it, and went through the whole story. Well, most of it. He left out a select few details about how he'd happened to be talking to Deborah in the wee hours of the morning.

"Me and Billy talked it over, Henry. We're gonna keep this under wraps, just like whoever it is doing this wants. But for a little different reason. We want them all to show themselves an' what they're up to before we go and do anything about it. So not a word, Henry. Not to anybody but the oldest and most dependable of our bunch. An' the boss don't even want you letting Dutch nor Smiley in on it by telegraph wire. If those boys from the Secret Service are in on the deal—if they really are from the Secret Service, that is—there's no telling what-all they might find out, right down to private telegraph messages. You know? So any word going out, it's gotta be face-to-face an' only with the few we know for certain sure we can trust. An' that *don't* include anybody, not one swinging dick, from the U.S. attorney's office or any of the politicians, not state nor federal level either one. You understand, Henry? Nobody but the boys we know are straight an' square an' loyal to Billy Vail. Not nobody else. None.''

"I understand," Henry said. "One thing, though."

"Yes?"

"Can I sneak in to see Billy?"

"We talked about that, Henry. Right now Billy don't think that would be safe. I only got in my own self by pretending to be a doctor, but we can't throw in too many fake doctors or somebody is gonna twig to the act. For right now you'd best stay away. What I think I'll do, though, an' this just now come to me, what I think I'll do is get my nurse friend to slip messages in or out as need be.''

"But wouldn't that mean taking her into our confidence? Are you sure we can trust her?''

"We already *are* relying on her when you think about it. She already knows this is a put-up deal, that there's secrets afoot. After all, her recognizing Billy an' thinking that surely I was a part of the conspiracy is what led me to Billy to start with. I mean, she knows it's taking place with Billy's cooperation. She doesn't know, an' doesn't have to at this point, that he was fooled into it. An' she won't say anything out of school. She only talked to me because she knows how close me and Billy are. She just naturally assumed I'd know what was going on, but she's no dummy. She likely figured out at least a part of the truth from the questions I was asking her so's I could get inside.

"The point is, she knows Billy and she trusts me. She won't do nothing to give us away. Best of all, she can walk into that room any time and the guards won't think a thing about it. She's been doing that ever since Billy was brought in. The guards won't know the difference between her going in there on a doctor's orders or on ours. They're used to seeing her in there two, three times every day. I'll get her to sneak in a pad of paper and some pencils—no sense trying to hide pens an' ink an' all that—so Billy can send instructions out if he wants to. Or whatever."

"I just wish . . . never mind," Henry said. "I can be patient if I have to."

"Sorry, but me and Billy talked about this. He thinks it's best for you to stay away. Me too unless there's damn good reason to play doctor again. And anyway, this idea of mine about Deborah will let us communicate. Billy can run things while whoever is behind this thinks they still got him isolated. That way they won't get scared off before we can finger them and figure out what they're up to."

"All right, Long. I'm in. Of course."

"Hell, Henry, I never for a minute thought you wouldn't be."

Henry nodded. "Do you still want that information about the driver and footman on the carriage?"

"Damn right I do. I asked Billy about it this morning, but he said he never got a look at whoever it was that threw the bomb. Said all he could see from where he was sitting in the front corner of the coach was somebody's hand. And they were wearing a glove at that. He saw the hand and the bomb and saw the thing bounce on the floor an' roll under Mrs. Troutman's dress."

"God!" Henry exclaimed. "That sounds terrible."

"Which it was, of course, but I expect that's what saved Billy's life. That poor woman took the full force of the explosion. She shielded the others from the blast with her flesh. It musta been an awful way to die. But quick. At least it woulda been quick.''

Henry reached into his coat and extracted a single sheet of paper. ''Here are the names you wanted, also the address of the company the men are employed by. The carriage was hired, of course.''

''D'you know by who?''

''Whom.''

''What?''

''Never mind. No, I don't know who hired them.''

''Reckon that's another thing I'll want to ask then.''

''Do you think that might be significant?''

Longarm shrugged. ''Henry, I got no damn idea what's gonna prove to be important or what won't. 'Bout all we can do at this point is commence stirring the water an' see what comes up mud.''

''Good luck, my friend. And in case you had any doubts, your news has made this a much better day than I ever expected it could be.'' Henry grinned and, walking with a much more lively and bouncy step than when he'd arrived, headed back toward the Federal Building.

There went one almighty happy man, Longarm thought with considerable pleasure of his own.

Chapter 28

E. P. Lewis and Co. was located on the outer fringes of town at the west end, a collection of ramshackle barns and corrals set in a grove of mature cottonwoods that grew beside a tiny creek. Most of the livestock appeared to be heavy workhorses, not fancy lightweights like those Longarm had seen hitched to the carriage that awful day outside the Federal Building.

That had been a matched set of grays. Four of them in showy, bright polished harness and purple plumes. Longarm looked in the corrals, but was sure none of the grays was on the premises now. He hoped they were not out on a job this morning. Not that he gave a damn about the horses particularly, but generally men and animals were matched in teams, so if the horses were gone there was a good chance the men might not be available either.

Still, he'd come this far. He did not intend to go back to the city without learning what he could here. He told the hack driver to wait for him—he did not want to have to walk back to the nearest point where he might reasonably expect to find another mode of transportation— and began poking through the various sheds and out-buildings in search of someone to talk to.

Most of the equipment in inventory consisted of heavy drays and freight wagons. Apparently the bulk of the company's business was commercial by nature, not just fancy outfits offered to the gentry.

The E. P. Lewis and Co. office turned out to be lodged in one of the barns, in a room originally intended to hold grain or harness or whatever.

"Would you be Mr. Lewis?" Longarm asked the young man in sleeve garters and eye protector that he found bent over a desk there.

"I would. Edward Charles Lewis, proprietor."

Longarm glanced down at the sheet of paper Henry had given him earlier. "I thought it was E. P. Lewis," he observed.

"That is the company name, yes. Edward Prentice Lewis was my father. He turned the business over to me two years ago and retired. Said it was my turn to support him for a change. Is there something I can do for you, sir?"

Longarm introduced himself.

"Ah, yes. I was wondering how long it would be before someone came around to ask about the tragedy."

"You haven't talked to anybody else before me?" Longarm asked.

"No, Marshal, you are the first."

That didn't sound right. Surely anyone interested in getting to the truth would want to talk to those who were actually at the scene. And as soon as possible too, before memories began to fade or, worse, be replaced with speculation gone over so often that the line dividing truth from imagination would begin to blur. Longarm found it odd that none of the investigators on the case had been there before now. Odd to say the least.

He said nothing about that to young Ed Lewis, of course. "I hope we'll be able to count on your cooperation," was all he said aloud.

"Certainly," Lewis assured him. "Mine and that of any of my people. Sit down, Marshal. Would you like some coffee? Or something stronger?"

"Nothing, thanks, but do you mind if I smoke in here?"

"In here no, but . . ."

"I won't carry it out into the barn with me," Longarm assured him, pulling out a pair of cheroots and offering one to Lewis, who declined the invitation.

Longarm took his time trimming and lighting the slender cigar, keeping his attention on the young entrepreneur without being obvious about it. Lewis seemed quite content to wait. He showed no nervousness or irritation whatsoever, but waited patiently for his guest to get on with the interview.

"I notice that the horses you used that day aren't in the corrals now. I hope them and the gents who were driving them aren't off working somewhere."

"The grays are gone because I had to sell them," Lewis told him. "The explosion ruined them. High-quality carriage horses have to be steady, you see. It is remarkable how exacting some customers can be, with the demands they sometimes place on horses and people alike. The grays were my best team, I have to tell you, but after the explosion they were not the same. Not dependable, you see. Why, we had to lip-twitch them or ear them down just to get harness onto them. They would not work together any longer, wouldn't stand without becoming nervous and working up a sweat. I felt sorry for the poor things, but I could no longer use them. I had to sell them off. Not as a team either, unfortunately, which cut into whatever value they should have had."

"Sorry to hear that," Longarm said. "What about the men?" Again he consulted Henry's slip of paper. "John Boatwright and Carl Beamon?"

"Boatwright was the driver of my carriage that day,"

Lewis said. "He is due to come on duty at noon. That will be in, what, forty-five minutes or so? Boatwright has a short hire for this afternoon with a light team. You can talk to him when he shows up for work. He is quite dependable; you can count on him being here when he said he would. Or if you prefer, I can give you his address and you can try to catch him at home, although he may already have gone somewhere for his dinner. He is a bachelor and generally takes his meals out," Lewis said.

"I'll see him here if it's all right with you."

"Of course. As for Beamon, I am afraid he is no longer available. He was killed, you see."

"Nobody told me he was hurt too," Longarm said.

"Oh, he was not injured in the explosion. It was practically a miracle the way he escaped that without harm. No, Carl died two days ago in an accident."

"Really."

"Yes. He was crossing the street. At night, although not particularly late. I am told he was on his way home after supper. He may have been drinking. I wouldn't know about that. In any event, a runaway wagon ran right over him when he stepped off the sidewalk. Broke his neck, I believe."

"This happened two nights ago?"

"That's right."

"Here?"

"In Aurora. Carl lived in Aurora."

"Uh-huh."

"It was a shame, of course. He was a good enough employee. Not as dependable as some, but better than most of the help I see here. I am still looking for a replacement. Uh, if you know of anyone . . ."

"Sorry, but I couldn't say that I do. Before I forget, Mr. Lewis, do you recall who it was that hired you to carry the commissioner and his party that day?"

"Yes, of course I do. The hire was arranged by the

United States attorney, a Mr. Terrell. I, um, don't suppose you know who I should contact about the bill for, uh, services rendered, do you? With Mr. Terrell among the casualties I haven't been sure. . . ."

Longarm wasn't about to tell this fellow that Terrell had survived the incident. "The acting U.S. attorney now is a man name of J. B. Cotton. You could try billing him. Or the office. I don't know if the hire was official government business or political. If it was s'posed to be political, then I expect you'd have to see some of the party officials. Whoever they might be."

"Yes, well, I guess I can try the official route first, and go to the party if that doesn't work." He frowned. "I shouldn't want to bill the estate. Someone needs to pay, although my insurance carrier will take care of at least partial replacement cost for the carriage. It was completely destroyed."

"Yes, sir, I was there that day. I saw what little was left of your rig."

Lewis shook his head. "All I saw was the aftermath. That was bad enough."

"Yes, sir." Longarm crossed his legs and ground out the coal of his cheroot on the sole of his boot, then tucked what was left of the smoke into a pocket. "Thanks for your time, Mr. Lewis. If I have more questions later . . ."

"You are welcome here any time, Marshal. Always glad to help the law, you know."

"Thank you, sir."

"As for Boatwright, talk to him all you need. If you want him for the afternoon, just say so and I will get someone else to take his place this afternoon."

"That won't be necessary, sir, but I appreciate your help. It won't go unnoticed."

"Any time, Marshal. Any time at all."

"Thank you, sir. Good day now." Longarm touched the brim of his Stetson and left the young man to his ledgers.

Chapter 29

"Remember it, mister? God, I reckon. I'll be able to call that day back to mind for the rest of my life, believe me," John Boatwright—"just call me Boats"—said when Longarm posed his question. "Who'd you say you are again, mister?"

Longarm dragged out his badge to flash, and repeated his name.

"I been expecting someone to ask me about it, of course," Boats said once he was satisfied that Longarm had an official right to be doing the asking.

"No one else has talked to you yet?" Longarm asked.

"A couple newspaper reporters. Snotty sons of bitches, they were. I didn't give them the time of day. Mr. Lewis, he said I didn't have to talk to them if I didn't want to. I asked him about that, see. He said it was all right."

"They came here to interview you?" Longarm asked, wondering why young Lewis hadn't mentioned the visit.

"No, they found me at home one evening. Same evening Beamon was killed, actually. They came by my place that night."

"Together?" Longarm asked. "More than one of them, that is?"

"That's right. Two of them."

"From the same newspaper?"

Boats shrugged. "I don't recall what paper they said they was from. If they said at all. I just don't remember about that. Is it important?"

"No, I'm sure it isn't. It's just that you never really know what will turn out to be of interest when you get into something like this. It's just better to ask everything that pops into mind and sort it all out afterward."

"Yeah, I guess that makes sense."

"So you talked to these two reporters but not to any police or other investigators," Longarm said.

"That's right. Until now."

"Can you describe these reporters?"

Boats proceeded to do so.

"Do you know if Carl Beamon was interviewed?" Longarm asked.

"Oh, I wouldn't know a thing like that, Marshal. Me and Beamon worked together sometimes, but we wasn't close. We wasn't what you'd call friends. Just coworkers. Me, I wouldn't have wanted to be seen in public dressed in a silly outfit like that rig Beamon used to dress up in, but he thought it made him look like somebody special. I thought it was stupid."

Longarm remembered the outfit. Livery, they called it. If pushed on the subject he would have had to throw in with Boatwright about it, though. It looked stupid, and would have been damn-all embarrassing to have to wear out in public. Kind of like a party costume but worse, since nobody else would be dressed up too.

"Are you willing to tell me what you remember about that day?" Longarm asked.

"Oh, sure. For whatever it's worth, which I guess wouldn't be much. I was sitting on top of the driving box holding the lines. Not that I expected any trouble from the horses. That was a real fine team until the explosion ruined them. But when you're dealing with rich folks you don't want to take any chances, if you know what I mean. Most people that pay for real fancy service want extra good service too. They don't want the team dragging the carriage out of place when they're trying to get aboard, nothing like that.''

Longarm nodded encouragement for Boats to continue.

"Beamon had got down to put out the steps and help the passengers in. That was his job, see. Mine was to drive and keep the horses nice and quiet. His was to coddle the paying passengers and make them feel the hire was worth what they paid for it. Pamper them. You know?''

Longarm nodded again.

"Anyway, Beamon was standing down there beside the rig. I was up top, just sitting there looking around. Mostly I was paying attention to my team's ears. That's the first thing you notice if there's gonna be trouble. They'll lay their ears flat, maybe switch their tails some. So mostly I was watching for that. Not close, mind. The team was steady. But I was looking in that direction, not back toward the carriage. Didn't have to look down to see that everyone was on, you understand. That would be clear enough when Beamon put the steps away and got back onto the box with me. I wouldn't take up the slack in my lines until then, so there wasn't need for me to look back at my passengers. Besides, some of them don't like being gawked at by workingmen like me and Beamon. Some of them are pretty snooty.''

"I'm sure," Longarm agreed.

"The first I knew anything was wrong was when I heard a scream. I suppose that's what you would call it. A yelp. An alarm, sort of. Then, before there was time for that to hardly sink in, there was the sound of the explosion. My seat was lifted up underneath me like I was sitting on a horse that was bucking, not at all like I was on something solid and secure like a seat bench.

123

It was like the whole damn rig was being tossed into the air, and then the team bolted. Can't say that I blamed them for that.

"They were running practically before the sound of the explosion stopped, and I was trying to get them under control. I knew something bad had happened to the carriage. I mean, I wasn't sitting straight and level like I ought to be. The ass end of the carriage was slumped down. I didn't know until later that the whole back half of the thing was blown off and that the frame was dragging on the ground. All I knew at the time was that I would've fallen off the back of the seat if there hadn't been a backrest behind me. I was leaning so far backward, I had to hunch forward and try to get the team back under control.

"It was . . . I don't know how long before I managed that. Sort of. Got them stopped anyway, mostly by running them into some bushes. It wasn't so much that they were responding to my lines as that they didn't have no place else to run. Anyway, it got them stopped. It was only after that that I saw what damage had been done to the carriage. And to those passengers. God, that was awful. Just awful."

Longarm certainly had to agree with that. He too remembered all too clearly. "Were all the passengers dead at that time?" he asked, particularly interested in hearing how Boatwright would respond to that one.

"No, sir, they weren't. The one man had his leg blowed off, and he was bleeding like I wouldn't have thought any one human person could. I think he was already dead by the time the ambulance got there, but I couldn't swear to that. I think the other two men was still alive at the time. The woman, I never saw her body. I don't know where it was. Blown all apart so there wasn't enough left to look like a body maybe. I wouldn't know."

"But two of the men, at least, were still alive?"

Boats shrugged. "Like I said, I couldn't swear to it. It's the impression I got. The papers said they died at the hospital, I think. I can believe it. That was a terrible strong explosion. A bomb, the papers said the next day."

"But you didn't see the bomb itself nor who threw it?" Longarm asked.

"No, sir. Like I told you, I was looking toward the front, toward my horses. I never seen what happened down behind me."

"Did Beamon see it?"

"He was standing right there. I'm sure he must've seen something."

"Did he say anything to you about it?"

"Afterward, while we was leading the horses back in. They were so spooked by what happened that they wouldn't drive again, Marshal. We tried and tried, but we couldn't get them to mind worth a damn. We ended up having to borrow another rig and lead them back here. Anyway, while we was doing that, Beamon talked a little. Not much, though. He was shaken up damn near as bad as those horses were. I'd ask him things and it was like he didn't hear."

Longarm remembered Billy saying that his hearing had been affected by the explosion, that he literally could not hear anything for several days afterward. It was entirely possible that Carl Beamon had not heard his partner's questions that afternoon.

"We was sitting side by side on the tailgate of the rig that was taking us home, each of us holding onto lead ropes for two of the grays. Sitting right side by side, but Beamon didn't really say all that much. He kept mumbling something, more like he was talking to himself than like he was trying to tell it to me. Said something like . . . let me think now . . . something like, 'Why'd she do that? Why'd she do that?' Over and over he kept repeating that. 'Why'd she do that?' I guess he must've been talking about the woman that was killed. She must've done something . . . I don't know . . . tried to protect her husband by throwing herself onto the bomb . . . something like that maybe. I asked Beamon a couple times what he meant, but he never answered. Like I said, he just sat there and acted like he didn't hear anything I said to him the whole rest of that afternoon.

"Then once we got back here to the barn and put the team up, we told Mr. Lewis what happened. He could see we were shaken up pretty bad, Beamon even more than me. He said we should take the next few days off and not come back in to work until we felt up to it. He's good about things like that, Mr. Lewis is. He's a good boss. Nice man.

"Anyway, we went our different ways, Beamon and me. I never saw him nor talked to him again. Next thing I knew . . . I was already back to work by then although he hadn't come in again yet . . . next thing I knew we were told about him having that accident and getting himself killed. Run over he was. Crazy, isn't it? He stands there right next to a bomb going off and doesn't have so much as a scratch on him. Then he goes to cross the damn street and gets run over by a wagon. It's crazy, I tell you. Crazy damn world sometimes."

"It is that," Longarm agreed. He reached for two cheroots, gave one to Boatwright, and shared a match with the man. "Is there anything else you can think of?"

"No, sir, I think that pretty much is everything I can remember," Boatwright responded.

"If you do think of anything more, no matter now insignificant it seems, I'd really appreciate it if you would tell me. Better yet, since I won't be spending much time in the office until this investigation is completed, if you think of anything you can come in and tell the clerk in the United States marshal's office. That's inside the Federal Building there, the same place you were picking those passengers up that day. Or you can drop me a note there. You remember my name?"

"Marshal Long, isn't it?"

"That's right. If you remember anything more, anything at all, you can write me a note and send it to me at the U.S. marshal's office, Federal Building, Denver, Colorado. It will reach me."

"I'll do it, Marshal. That's a promise."

Longarm thanked the man, shook his hand, and went to reclaim his hack. The charge for so much waiting around was sure to be high, but he figure it was money well spent.

He just wished the time had been better spent. It was a lousy break that Boatwright hadn't been paying attention to the passengers at that moment, but his account of things certainly made sense. It was a much worse break that Carl Beamon was dead and could no longer be interviewed. Dammit.

"Where to, mister?" the hack driver asked when Longarm climbed into the hired rig.

"Aurora," Longarm told him. "I want to go to the Aurora City Hall."

"You got it, mister."

Longarm could practically hear the man's thoughts as he calculated how much this fare was going to end up being. One customer like Longarm could make a hackney driver's whole day.

The driver snapped his whip over his team's ears, and the wagon lurched into motion, throwing Longarm against the back of the seat. Next stop Aurora, way the hell and gone on the east side of Denver.

Chapter 30

"Come have lunch with me, Thaddeus. I'm buying."

"Now that isn't an offer that comes along every day, Longarm. You want something, don't you?" the assistant police chief of the city of Aurora accused him with a grin.

"Hell, yes, I want something. D'you think I'd waste money on an ugly old fart like you if I didn't?"

Thad Browne laughed. Then he stood and reached for his coat and hat. "I'll tell the desk sergeant where to find me, then we're gone. Will Finch's Chop House be all right?"

"Any place you say."

"Any place? You really do want something, don't you. I think I probably should have suggested someplace more expensive. Would have if I'd known this beforehand."

"If you want to change your mind . . ."

"Jim Finch would be offended if I ate anywhere else. Probably spit in my food the next time I came in. Can't allow that, can I? Otherwise I'd see if I couldn't bust your bank, by Godfrey."

Longarm laughed and followed his old friend out of the Aurora police station. He and Browne had known each other for years and got along almighty well.

Longarm had been to Finch's before, always with Thad Browne. The Aurora cop ate there nearly every day and was a fixture at the place. It was, however, a good enough choice, quiet, with excellent food and a selection of the dark beers that Browne preferred. They also, Longarm remembered, stocked a superior-quality rye whiskey that never failed to please Longarm's palate.

Browne did not have to bother telling the waiter what he wanted. Neither his beverage nor his food order ever varied. Longarm decided on his own selection from the menu posted on a slate chalkboard, then waited for the waiter to get out of hearing distance before he brought up the reason for his visit.

"Carl Beamon. Do you remember the case, Thad?"

"Certainly. Hit by a runaway freight wagon while he was crossing the street."

"Anything unusual about the case?" Longarm asked.

"Not really. Officially it could be a crime, of course, because the driver didn't stop or come back to see how badly the man was injured. But I wouldn't necessarily call it unusual just because of that. The driver would only claim loss of control anyway, and if he heard afterward that the man was killed, he wouldn't want to admit to it. He could end up charged with manslaughter if anyone wanted to press the issue. At the least he would be vulnerable to a lawsuit by the survivors, if any. Which isn't to say that I condone the silence, but it is common enough. Understandable."

"I suppose so."

"We deal with a different class of criminal from what you do, old friend. One learns to be practical about which laws you enforce and what you just let slide. This one . . ." Browne shrugged and gave Longarm a look that was not especially apologetic. It was simply the way things were. Longarm was glad he was a federal peace officer, not a local copper.

The waiter returned with their drinks, and Browne toasted Longarm with a salute of his beer stein, then drained off nearly half the foamy liquid in a single pull. Longarm returned the favor with the tumbler of whiskey he'd been given—no picayune shot glasses here, thank you—and was reminded anew of how good the rye was at Finch's. If only everyone served whiskey this smooth, the world would be a better place.

"What's your interest in Beamon, Longarm?"

"He was the footman on the carriage when Billy and those others were killed. I wanted to talk to him to find out if he saw anything that would be helpful."

"Really? I didn't know that."

"Beamon was standing right beside the door when somebody tossed that bomb into the carriage. He must have seen something. Must have."

"Too late now to ask him," Thad said sympathetically. "I guess he didn't tell the official investigators anything, though, or you wouldn't be here now."

"That's right." There seemed no point in mentioning that as far as Longarm knew, no official investigators had ever tried to speak with Beamon. "I take it you already know that I'm not on the case. Officially, that is."

"Word does get around, you know. Not that I can say I agree with the decisions that are being made over there. I can see the logic, I suppose. But I disagree with the conclusions. It's all a matter of inexperience, I presume."

"I s'pose," Longarm said.

"But unofficially?"

"I expect you know the answer to that."

"Billy was a fine man. The best," Browne said. "It won't be easy to replace him."

"No," Longarm agreed. It was hard as hell keeping his mouth shut about the truth. Dammit, they could trust Thad. Longarm would have bet his life on that. But who

130

might Thad let it slip to if he knew Billy and the others were still alive? And could that unknown third party be trusted? That was the problem. There just wasn't any choice about it. Longarm had to keep his mouth shut. And apologize to Thad later, when it would be safe to tell rest of the truth.

"Will you apply for the job?"

"Not me, Thad. I'm not no administrator."

"I was thinking I might dip a toe into the water, see if a fish rises to it."

"Go ahead," Longarm said.

Browne grinned. "You'd have a helluva time if I was your boss, Deputy Long. Might have to work for a living and everything."

"I'd hate that," Longarm said. "It'd be kinda different, though, wouldn't it."

Thad laughed.

"Anything else you can tell me about Carl Beamon?"

"Not really. Nothing special anyway."

"Was he a drinking man?"

"No, not really."

"But he'd been drinking some that evening, had he?"

"He'd had a few, I'm told. I don't think he was drunk if that's what you mean."

"Did he live alone? Have a wife? Anyone he might've talked to about the bombing before he died?"

"He had a girlfriend, I think. Look, why don't we go back to my office after lunch. I'll pull the reports on this and you can look them over. Anything my officers found out will be in there. I'm particular about the paperwork, you know."

"Which is why you make a good administrator an' why I wouldn't't," Longarm said.

"Ah. It looks like our lunch is ready. Get out your purse, my friend. I intend to have another beer. Maybe two or three."

"Good. The drunker you get, Browne, the more I can pry outa you."

"Hell, I'm willing."

Longarm chuckled. And ordered another rye whiskey. He pretty much had to if he wanted to keep pace with his friend. And it would have been damn-all rude to do otherwise.

Chapter 31

BethAnne Mobley wasn't home when Longarm first called at her apartment looking for her. "She works days, mister, and is gone most nights too," the next-door neighbor told him. "Try again about supper time. You might could catch her then."

Rather than going all the way back to Denver and then returning to Aurora in the evening, Longarm marked time in a billiards parlor until shortly before six, then once more went to the home of Carl Beamon's reputed girlfriend.

This time his knock was answered by a pale, very thin girl with huge eyes and a vapid, vacant expression. "Who do you want? Carl? He isn't here, mister. Carl is dead."

"I know that, miss. It's you I wanted to talk with. About him."

"Me? What for?"

"Could I come inside, miss? I think it would be best if we didn't stand in the hallway discussing this."

The girl shrugged and backed away from the door, allowing Longarm inside.

Her apartment was shabby, the furnishings cheap to begin with, and not helped any by having been in service years longer than they should have been. The place was unkempt, soiled clothing littering practically every flat surface in the place and a sour smell coming from the tiny alcove that served as a kitchen. Longarm had seen dog kennels he would rather have lived in. BethAnne did not seem to notice, certainly did not offer any apologies.

"Who'd you say you are, mister?" she asked.

He repeated the introduction and said, "I want to talk with you about Carl Beamon. He was your boyfriend, is that correct?"

BethAnne snorted. "That's what he told people anyhow. Wasn't true, though. I wasn't his girlfriend. Not like you'd think. We spent some time together. Carl was generous. You know?" She fashioned a bright, wide, and patently phony smile. "Are you generous, mister? Are you gonna buy me some of my medicine? Carl always did. Would you, please?"

BethAnne did not look particularly sick. "What medicine would that be, miss?"

"Delphium's Elixir is what I take, mister. For my pains. Female troubles is what it is. Delphium's helps. Carl always brought me Delphium's whenever he came to visit."

"We'll talk first," Longarm told her. "Then I'll get you some medicine." Delphium's Elixir was not a name he was familiar with, but he pretty much knew what to expect. The stuff would be one of those shady excuses for indulgence under the guise of medication. In truth it would be either alcohol under a fancy name or, worse, one of the opium derivatives. Either way, the object of taking it would be to dull, not simple pain, but the discomfort of a poor existence. Longarm had seen it often enough before. BethAnne Mobley was not the first he'd encountered who was addicted to her magic potion of choice, and he doubted she would be the last.

"You're just telling me that," she said. "If I tell you

what you want, you won't really get me my medicine."

"I will. I promise."

"For sure? You promise?"

He nodded. Hell, why not. The quack products weren't illegal. And if buying this vapid young woman some would help him find out more about the bombing, well, that was a small price to pay. He meant what he said.

BethAnne smiled then and fingered the buttons at the front of her dress. Quickly, before the stupid little cunt had time to offer more than conversation in return for her drug, Longarm said, "I want you to tell me everything Carl Beamon told you about the bombing he was involved in last week."

The girl frowned. "Oh, yeah. That. I remember he did say something about that. But I . . . it's all sort of fuzzy in my mind. You know?"

"Try to remember, please. It's important."

"You'll really and truly buy me a bottle of Delphium's, mister?"

"I promise. Maybe two bottles."

That got her attention all right. BethAnne sat up straighter on the torn, worn-out upholstery of the chair she'd settled on. She smiled again. Her teeth were small and white and perfect.

"Carl got himself killed. Did I tell you that?"

"Yes, I heard. But what did he say about the bombing?"

"He said . . . let me think now."

Longarm was pretty sure he knew what she was thinking. BethAnne was trying to work out what she thought he wanted to hear. Whatever she decided that would be, that was what she would tell him.

"Just the truth, BethAnne. That's important. I'll buy you the Delphium's even if what you say isn't important. But I want you to understand that it is very important

135

that you tell me the truth. If you do that, then I promise to get you the Delphium's. All right?"

"Sure, mister. Okay."

"Do you remember what it was that Carl told you after the bombing?" He wasn't sure this girl was consistently capable of remembering her own name. But he had to try. BethAnne might well be the only avenue he would ever have into Carl Beamon's memories of that day. He had to ask her.

"I think . . . look, mister, this don't sound like much. Okay?"

"It's all right no matter what it is, just so long as it is true. I promise."

"Yeah, well, all I remember Carl saying . . . I mean, he didn't come here to talk, really. He was sweet on me, you know? He practically loved me. That's why he always told people he was my boyfriend. I mean, he knew better. But he liked to sort of believe it himself and he told everybody that. I guess I shoulda been mad at him, but I wasn't. I thought it was kinda cute. You know?"

"Sure. So what was it he said?"

"He came by like he usually did after he'd got some work. He didn't have work every day, you know. When he did, he'd buy me my Delphium's and bring some by and then we'd spend a little time together and then he'd go home. So anyway, this one night he came by and he gave me my Delphium's like always, but this one night, he wasn't interested in . . . you know, the usual stuff. I mean, he didn't even try to do anything. I don't know that he could have done it if he'd tried, he was that upset. He just brought me my bottle and fixed me some tea with the elixir in it, and then he wanted to just kinda sit and talk. Except he wasn't making much sense. It was more like he was talking to himself than to me. You know what I mean, mister?"

"Sure, BethAnne. It's like that sometimes. D'you remember what it was Carl was saying to himself that night?''

''It didn't make no sense.''

''That's all right. Tell me anyway, please.''

''Well, first off he kept saying over and over, 'Why'd she do that? Why'd she go and do that?' Something like that.''

''And then?''

''Then later on he said . . . a couple different times, I guess it was . . . he said, 'She was so pretty. Who would of thought a pretty girl like that would go and do something like she done.' '' BethAnne frowned as if in concentration. ''Does that make sense to you, mister?''

''No,'' he admitted. ''I can't say that it does.''

''Not to me neither.''

''Was there anything else?''

BethAnne shook her head. ''That was the last time I talked to Carl. No, it wasn't. No, sir, it wasn't for a fact. That was the last time Carl came to visit me. But a couple days after that, I think it was, I ran into him at the pharmacy where I get my medicine. Another gentleman was nice enough to give me money so I could buy myself some Delphium's and I'd gone to the store to do that, and I ran into Carl there. I thought he was there to buy me some Delphium's, that he'd be by to see me that night. I asked him if he was coming over, but he said no, he wouldn't be able to do that, that he had to meet a couple fellas that wanted to talk to him.''

She frowned again. ''What else did he say? There was something . . . oh, yeah. Now I remember. He said after he talked to these two men he would have lots of money. He said he could buy me a whole case of Delphium's then if I wanted. Of course I didn't believe him. But it was kinda sweet of him to say so anyhow. Carl wasn't usually a tease like that. I don't know why he would of said any such thing that time.''

''But he didn't come by again?'' Longarm asked.

"No, of course not. That was the same day he got killed. That same afternoon. I'm pretty sure it was."

It was Longarm's turn to frown. "You're sure he said he was going to meet two men?"

"Yeah, that's what he said. Two of them."

"He didn't say who they were or what they wanted?"

"No. Just that he was going to meet these two men and then he'd have lots of money and he'd buy me a bunch of my medicine and him and me could have a real long party. He wanted me to go off somewhere with him. He'd mentioned that a bunch of times before, but he'd never had money enough to make good on it. He said he would this time." She sighed. "But I never saw him again after that afternoon. Look, mister, you aren't gonna forget what you promised, are you?"

"No." Longarm smiled and stood up, reaching for his Stetson. "I tell you what, BethAnne. Show me where you get your medicine and I'll get it for you now. Would that be all right?"

She gave him another of those bright, perfect, utterly insincere smiles. "Would you like to have a little party first, mister? I wouldn't mind. Honest. You're handsome and you look clean. And I don't look like so much, but I can move it real good, and that's the natural truth. I'd drain you so good. . . ."

"Thanks, BethAnne. You're a mighty pretty girl, and I'm awful tempted," he lied. "But it's against the law for me to mess with a witness. I could lose my job if I did anything like you say, and the both of us might go to jail."

"Oh, gosh, mister. They wouldn't give me my medicine if I was in jail, would they?"

"No, I don't think they'd allow Delphium's Elixir in the jail, BethAnne."

The overlarge smile flickered and was replaced by one

138

that was not quite so big but that at least looked sincere this time. "Can we go get that medicine now, please?"

"Sure, BethAnne. Show me where, and I'll buy it for you."

Chapter 32

Longarm was so tired he felt like he might fall over sideways at any moment. And if he did he would likely start to snore and not wake up until tomorrow morning. What with the visit to Deborah last night, and then going out to see Billy with his very own eyes, he hadn't gotten a wink. And he was damn sure starting to feel it. He had to get some sleep soon or his eyeballs might drop clean out of his face. They already felt gritty and burned like a pair of coals in a dying fire.

But, dammit, he wasn't done there in Aurora yet. He still knew too damn little about Carl Beamon and what the man might have seen that day the bomb went off.

BethAnne Mobley had been a help. More so than she realized. But surely there was more to it than Beth-Anne's confused and muddied mind was able to recall.

Then Longarm had a stroke of genius—if he did say so his own damn self—and headed for the boarding-house where Beamon had lived.

"Ma'am," Longarm said to the tall, rather hefty woman who opened the door to his knock. "Could I put up here for a single night?"

"My rate is four dollars for the week."

"I only need the one night."

"I don't run a hotel here, young man. I offer rooms by the week or by the month. No exceptions."

"I could pay a dollar and a half for the one night, ma'am. You do include board, don't you?"

She sniffed. "You could put up at the hotel over on Main for half that."

"But they wouldn't have meals as good as what I've heard you serve."

"Who told you that, young man?" It had been a hell of a long time since he'd been called that.

"Fella name of . . . let me think . . . Beamon? Something like that."

"He boarded with me, that's true enough. Are you a friend of his?"

"An acquaintance is all," Longarm said, "but he spoke highly of you. That's why I thought of you when I discovered I have to stay over tonight. Your people haven't finished with supper yet, have they?"

"A dollar and a half, you say. Cash money?"

"Yes, ma'am."

"I would have to wash the sheets after only one night's use, you know."

"I could go as high as a dollar seventy-five. My boss won't reimburse me for anything more than that."

"You're a businessman, Mister . . . ?"

"Long," Longarm told her with a smile. "Custis Long."

"My name is Willets. Missus Willets, if you please."

"Yes, ma'am."

"You don't have luggage, Mr. Long?"

"No, ma'am. I didn't expect to be staying over."

"Yes, well, you seem a nice man, Mr. Long. I am willing to make an exception for you. Come inside. Supper will be served in twenty minutes. There is a pump and wash basin on the back porch, clean towels in the pantry. One towel and one change of linen each week. Not that that applies to you, of course."

"Yes, ma'am, thank you, ma'am." He touched the brim of his Stetson and went inside to join the men who had been Carl Beamon's friends. Or so, at least, he hoped.

Chapter 33

It was no wonder Mrs. Willets was so impressed by a compliment to her food that she agreed to make an exception to her rules for the man who gave it. Longarm was fairly sure the poor soul had never before received any compliments on her cooking. If only because none were warranted.

The food was, to be charitable, lousy. Bland and cheap, without even the saving grace of being greasy. And all of it pretty much the same pale gray color, boiled meat included. A man had to be mighty hungry in order to force the shit into his face. Fortunately Longarm was plenty hungry. He finished his first plateful and, to Mrs. Willets's obvious approval, asked for seconds. None of the other fellows at the table competed with him in a scramble for refills.

"Save room for dessert, Mr. Long," Mrs. Willets helpfully advised.

"Oh, I'll surely do that, ma'am, thank you." He smiled at the old battle-ax and had some more lumpy mashed potatoes swimming in an off-white liquid that was either gravy or library paste, he wasn't quite sure which.

Dessert turned out to be bread pudding lightly laced

with small black lumps that he almost desperately hoped were raisins. They must have been, he concluded, because the other boarders, who should already be wise to the potential dangers of Mrs. Willets's table, all dug into the bread pudding without restraint, although several of them had passed up certain of the earlier courses.

When he was done filling the aching void that had been in his stomach, Longarm pushed back from the table, thumped the flat of his belly, and asked, "Anybody care to join me in a cigar after dinner? I have enough to spare."

"I'll take you up on that offer, mister," one man said. "Me too."

"You may smoke on the front porch, Mr. Long," Mrs. Willets announced firmly. "Please do not light up until you are outside."

"Yes, ma'am," he said, docile as a lamb and twice as innocent.

The two smokers in the crowd led the way from the dining room onto the porch, Longarm following close behind. Once outside, Longarm's excellent cheroots in hand and streaming wisps of pale smoke, the men introduced themselves. Thomas Carey and Bernard Hicks, they said they were. The names meant nothing to Longarm. Apparently there had been no reason to mention either of them in the report Thad Browne's coppers had prepared in the wake of the accident that killed Carl Beamon.

"What brings you to Aurora, Mr. Long?"

"Where are you from?"

Longarm smiled at the two and told them, "Business, Mr. Hicks. And I'm from real far away." He blew a smoke ring. "All the way from Denver." He laughed. "Had to stay overnight and picked this place on the recommendation of a fella I met once. Carl Beamon? Either of you know him?"

"We did," Hicks said.

"Did? What'd he do, move out?"

"He's dead," Tom Carey informed the newcomer.

"No shit," Longarm said with feigned surprise. "What happened?"

"Just an accident," Carey said.

"Bullshit," Hicks disagreed. "Carl was murdered, and that's a fact."

"Murdered?" Longarm prompted.

"He was."

"Mr. Long, don't believe that. Beamon died in an accident. Just a runaway wagon."

"He was murdered," Hicks insisted.

"It was an accident."

"What makes you think it was murder, Mr. Hicks?"

"I don't think it was, I know it was. Carl—I knew him better than anyone else here—Carl told me he was going to come into some big money. He was supposed to meet two men that evening, see. He knew something important, and these men he was meeting, they were going to pay him to tell them about it. But only them. That was the deal. They wanted him to tell them everything he knew, but agree to not tell anyone else."

"Did he tell you what it was that he knew, what it was that was so important?"

Hicks shook his head. "He said he couldn't. Not if he wanted the money."

"Mr. Long, my friend Bernie here has a real vivid imagination. Don't believe any of this. Beamon was killed in an ordinary, everyday kind of accident. That's what the police said, and who would know better than them?"

That was a question Longarm was not inclined to get into at the moment. If he ever did, though, Tom Carey might be in for some rude awakenings.

"So who were these two men?" Longarm asked. "Did he meet with them before he was killed? Did he have money on him when he died?"

Carey scowled and said, "I don't want to be rude, mister, but I don't want to listen to any more of this. Good night, the both of you." Carey went back inside the boardinghouse, leaving Longarm and Hicks alone on the porch. Longarm settled into a rocking chair and motioned for Hicks to join him in a companion chair nearby.

"You really believe Beamon was murdered, don't you?"

"I do, sir. Like I said, I knew Carl better than anyone else here. He was genuinely excited about his good fortune, about coming into some money. I don't know how much these men had talked about paying him, but it must have been some hundreds of dollars anyway. That would have been very big money indeed for someone like Carl. Or for that matter for someone like me. I know I've never made more than eight dollars in one week, not in my whole life. I doubt Carl ever made that much even."

"Who were these men? Police? Reporters? Something like that?" The men who spoke with Boatwright had introduced themselves as reporters. Two of them. Longarm's experience, though, was that genuine reporters seldom traveled in pairs. Generally they were loners interested in being the first to get the news, competing even with others working for the same newspaper or magazine. Two men had talked to Boatwright. Two men were supposed to talk with Beamon. Longarm placed scant faith in coincidence at the best of times, and he saw no reason to suspend that skepticism now.

"I don't know," Hicks said. "Carl never told me that."

"Do you know where they were to meet him?"

"Yes, he did tell me that. They were meeting him at the Lone Tree Saloon."

That was interesting, Longarm thought. It was outside the Lone Tree that Beamon had died. And these two men, whoever they were, knew to expect Beamon to be at that place, presumably at that time. It would have been no particular trick to fake a runaway and deliberately run someone down in the street. It was the sort of thing that could be done in plain sight of half the town's population and no one would know it was no accident.

"Did Carl mention anything to you about a girl?" Longarm asked. "A pretty girl? Something that had to do with the bombing he escaped a few days before he died?" That clue was one BethAnne Mobley had unknowingly given him. A pretty girl who Beamon had talked about, a pretty girl who had done something. Longarm had seen Commissioner Troutman's wife. No one in his right mind would have termed her a pretty girl. Probably not even when she'd been young enough to qualify as a girl, and that had been one hell of a long time back.

"No, he didn't. He never said anything like that. I'm sure of it."

"How about an Indian girl?" Longarm asked. "He never said anything to you about a pretty Indian girl?" The official line still maintained that the Utes were behind the bombing. If the bomb was thrown by a girl— one Longarm suspected Beamon might have seen and been talking about—he supposed it would not have been impossible that the girl was a Ute.

"An Indian? Absolutely not. Carl wouldn't have called Pocahontas a pretty girl. And if he'd seen an Indian he would surely have mentioned it. He was petrified of all Indians. Hated them too, but mostly he was scared of them. He couldn't stand to be near one. Not any Indian."

"Oh?"

"When he was a kid, eight, ten years old, something like that, his family was traveling overland from Ohio. They'd stopped beside some creek. He didn't know where. Kansas maybe, or Nebraska. I suppose it didn't really matter. Carl wandered off with some dough balls and a hand line to see if he could catch some fish. He hadn't hardly gotten out of sight from the camp than some Indians attacked. They killed everybody in his family. His father, his brothers, his mother and sister. Carl heard it happening. He hid in the brush. Stayed there for days, I guess, even after the Indians were long gone. It must've been terrible what they did to his mother and sister. He said afterward he wasn't sure which body was which, just that two of the bodies were female.

"He never knew what tribe it was that killed his people. Didn't matter to him. He was afraid of all Indians after that. Right to this day—that is, to the day he died, I guess. Scared to death of them. No, mister, if he saw an Indian, Carl never would have referred to her as being pretty.''

Longarm grunted and sat back in the rocker, digesting both the meal that lay heavy in his stomach and the information Bernie Hicks was telling him.

"I wish I knew what it was he was going to tell those two men," Longarm mused out loud.

"You aren't a businessman from Denver, are you, mister?''

Longarm smiled and confessed his occupation.

"That's all right then. I expect you have the right to know in that case.''

"You've been a big help, Mr. Hicks. Thank you.''

"I wish I could give you the rest of the answers, Marshal.''

"I wish you could too. But don't worry. We'll find out sooner or later. One way or some-damn-other. This is one murder that won't go unpunished. That's a promise. If you think of anything else that might be helpful . . .''

Hicks nodded. "I'll let you know.''

"Good. An' now, sir, I think I better get upstairs to

bed before I fall asleep right here in this chair an' don't wake again until breakfast.'' Longarm stood, yawning. ''Good night, Mr. Hicks.''

''Good night, Marshal.''

Chapter 34

A girl. The stinking sonuvabitch of a bomb was thrown
by a girl, and a pretty girl at that. *Not* an Indian girl.
Black hair or a black wig. Longarm had seen that for
himself that day. Not seen. Exactly. It was more like an
impression than any sight he could call precisely to mind
again. But he'd definitely had an impression of black
hair underneath the cape and hood of the bomber.

Cape and hood. And it was a damn girl. Shit, she
could've ducked round a corner and tossed the cape into
a trash can, then come right back and joined the crowd
of gawking blood-lookers who gathered in the aftermath
of every public tragedy.

Longarm could have stood beside her that day and
never known the difference. He, everybody, naturally
thought of the bomber being a man. For sure it had been
a man he'd gone dashing around looking for after the
explosion. A man with longish black hair. Likely an Indian. It was no damn wonder he hadn't seen anybody
like that. It was even luckier that there hadn't been some
poor innocent Indian wandering past that day. The Indian would have been strung up from a lamppost and
never deserved it. Hell, Longarm or one of the other
boys might well have shot him down their own selves

150

and felt righteous about it. And the truth was that it was some damn girl who did this.

Longarm grimaced. He needed to talk to Billy Vail again. That was all there was to it. He had to see Billy, never mind that contact between them was dangerous. Never mind that it might give the game away and alert whoever was behind this that Billy's boys were onto the lies.

Dammit, it was a chance they would just have to take.

But first there were a couple things Longarm wanted to do, a couple things he needed to set up. Then, dangerous or no, he would pay a call on "Mr. Janus" over at the hospital.

Satisfied that he was doing the right thing, Longarm left the boardinghouse that morning, lighted a cheroot, and went off in search of a hack to take him back to Denver. He had a lot to do, and the quicker he got to it the better it would be for all concerned.

"Do you know that every time I see that stupid hat I think there's some big-ass bird nesting in your hair."

Deborah laughed so hard she sprayed bits of bread crust onto her smock. "What are you doing here, Custis?" she asked as she brushed the crumbs off her breast. Longarm would gladly have volunteered to do that for her, but he doubted she would have let him. Not out here in broad daylight where half the doctors and nurses in Denver could see if they were of a mind to be looking. And who in their right mind would not be looking when the prettiest one of them all was sitting there on a shaded bench having her lunch? For certain sure it was a view Longarm enjoyed. Deborah smiled when he told her that. "Thank you. But I notice you haven't answered my question yet. What brings you here now? And why didn't you come by last night? I thought we were supposed to have supper at the Windemere."

Longarm winced. He'd forgotten about that. Hell, it

was only idle bed talk that had brought it up to begin with. He'd forgotten about it within seconds of suggesting it. "I was asleep when I told you we'd do that," he said, trying to wriggle off the hook. "I meant that we'd do it tonight, not last night. Last night I was working. Honest."

Deborah gave him a deliberately skeptical look, then relented and showed him a welcoming smile. "All right. I forgive you. On condition that you take me out to dinner tonight instead."

"That's a deal," Longarm promised.

"Now about that question I asked you . . ."

"I need a favor," he said.

"Somehow, Custis, that does not surprise me."

"I need to get in to see Billy again, Deb. Can you swipe a doctor's coat and whatever other stuff it will take to make me look like I belong here?"

"Of course. Better yet, I will go with you when you go to his room. A doctor and nurse together won't seem suspicious, but a strange doctor on the floor might."

Longarm thought that over and had to agree. Her idea was a good one. "Once we're inside an' I can talk with Billy without being overheard, there's something else I want you to do too. I need to know if there's any other rooms, on the other floors maybe, with guards outside them. I need to know if there's other patients who may be being hidden there like Billy is."

"You think the others might have survived too?"

"Two of them maybe."

Deborah shook her head. "There were only four people inside the carriage, right?"

"That's right."

"The lady was killed, of course. And at least one man. His leg was blown off, and if he didn't die at the scene he bled to death en route to the hospital. I was on duty that day, Custis. I am sure that he was declared dead on arrival. As for the fourth man—third, I mean, fourth person—I can't be so certain. But I can find out for you, of course. I'll take you in to see Billy first. Then I can check on this other man for you."

"You're a dóll. If we weren't in public I'd show you how much I appreciate you."

"Keep that in mind, dear. You can show me tonight." She smiled. "After dinner."

"Right. After dinner. It's a promise."

Deborah wrapped the remainder of her sandwich in a napkin and tucked it away in the tiny wicker basket she brought her lunch in each day, then stood and brushed her skirt off. "Ready?"

"When you are."

"Then follow me, Doctor."

Chapter 35

Billy's brows furrowed in intense concentration. Frustration too, more than likely. Longarm suspected his boss was having a perfectly awful time staying cooped up in here while there was work to be done out in the rest of the world. "A girl, you say? You think the bomb was thrown by a girl?"

"I can't prove it, Billy. The fellow who could have was killed in an accident that I'd have to say looks more an' more suspicious the more I look at it." Longarm relayed the information he'd learned about Carl Beamon and the two men who'd been expected to make him rich that same night the man was killed.

Billy grunted. "He talked about a girl throwing the bomb?"

"He talked about a girl. A pretty girl. He never exactly said that she's the one that threw the bomb. But that's the inference you pretty much have to make when you put the statements together. He told two, three different people that, or something like it. Kept mumbling about a girl. That's what the driver of the carriage said and the girlfriend"—it seemed kinder to refer to BethAnne as a girlfriend rather than the tawdry little cheap hooker she really was—"and the fellow at the

154

boardinghouse. He told all of them pretty much the same thing, but never got into any detail about it. And in truth he never actually said that this girl, whoever she was, was the one that threw the bomb into your carriage.''

"But why would some girl—not an Indian, but a white girl—why would she want to kill the commissioner?'' Billy mused aloud.

"I been wondering that too, Boss. Do you know what I asked myself? On the ride over here I got to thinking. We all been running in pretty much the same direction. We all been thinking in terms of someone that wanted to kill Commissioner Troutman. Billy, we don't know *why* somebody threw that bomb any more than we know *who*.''

"That's true,'' Billy agreed.

"Instead of concentrating on the obvious, Billy, maybe we oughta look at things from some other points of view. Like . . . is there anybody that might've wanted to kill you, for instance, and the commissioner just kinda got caught in the middle? I mean, it was a bomb, after all. Bombs ain't exactly specific about who they pick out to blow apart. An' I don't see it carved in stone anywhere that the thing had to be aimed at Commissioner Troutman. It could as easy have been you they wanted to kill an' got him by mistake.''

"You're really sure he is dead, Longarm?''

"Yes, sir. My nurse friend assures me the commissioner was dead when they carried him off that ambulance.''

"But they told me . . .''

"Yeah. I been thinking about that. Attorney Cotton and those politicians did tell you he was still alive. They have to've had a pretty good reason for wanting to make you believe that and for keeping you under wraps here all this time.''

"I can't imagine what that reason could be,'' Billy admitted.

155

"Neither can I just now. But we know there is a reason. Has to be a pretty damn good one too for them to go to all this trouble about it. Now that we know there's something to look for, I expect we'll figure it out eventually."

"I cannot believe those men would engage in a conspiracy to murder anyone," the marshal declared.

"No, sir. I been thinking about this plenty, as I expect you can imagine. I got to believe the same thing. Colorado politicians can be about as greedy an' nasty as the rest of 'em, but murder isn't usually one of their methods. Devious, sure. Lying, cheating, selfish, grab-with-both hands assholes, yes. But murderers? I don't think so. So I been kinda leaning toward another conclusion that I got no proof for whatsoever, Billy."

"Yes?"

"What I'm beginning to think, Boss, is that we got two different things going on here. I think somebody, for what they musta considered good reason, decided to throw that bomb at one or more of the people in that carriage. They wanted to kill somebody. Just exactly *which* somebody—or somebodies—remains to be seen. Then after they done that, Attorney Cotton and those other men, the state senator an' congressman and maybe others too, they jumped in with a plan of their own. Again we don't know why, but we do know that they're covering up the commissioner's death. At least to you, they are, though it was in all the newspapers and everywhere public that him and his wife were killed.

"What I got to think, Billy, is that these are two separate things, done for two different reasons, an' they aren't necessarily connected except by happenstance."

Billy pursed his lips and scratched his neck. He hadn't shaved in two days or more, and he was beginning to look a trifle on the scruffy side. Probably was starting to itch too. "It could be."

"Damn right it could."

"I can't think of anyone who had a reason to kill me," Billy admitted. "Nothing special anyway."

"All right. What about Mr. Terrell? Would anyone want him dead?"

"Not more than several hundred, I suppose. All I do is chase them. He is the one who puts them away."

"Anyone that he mentioned in particular lately?" Longarm asked.

Billy scratched some more. "He did mention one investigation that he intended to take before a special grand jury later this year."

"Yes?"

"Sedition, that one was. He said a group of anarchists were planning to disrupt the exercise of lawful authority in Colorado and several other Western states and territories."

"Anarchists?"

"That's right. Apparently there is a nest of them living on the north side, somewhere in those tenements north of the tenderloin district. Jason said they were mostly Middle Europeans. Serbs and Slavs, some Italians, I believe. We didn't talk about it too much. He only mentioned it so I could think about providing help with his investigations when the time came. I understand he had his own sources of information, some inside contact who was willing to inform on the others in the— what did he call it?—cell, I believe was the word he used. A cell of anarchists bent on destroying our form of government so they could replace it with what they refer to as 'man's natural state of self-reliance.' Some stupidity like that. You know the kind. No taxes, no controls, free love, all that horseshit. The whole bunch of them are probably lunatics."

"Fanatical lunatics?" Longarm asked.

"Could be," Billy said.

"Fanatic enough to throw a bomb that would wipe out not just the government officer who was a direct

157

threat to them but a friend of the president too?"

"It makes sense, in a manner of speaking."

"Yeah. Doesn't it."

"I think you should look into that," Billy said. "Look in Jason's files. There should be something there on the progress of his inquiries."

"All right, Boss. I damn sure will," Longarm promised. "First thing."

Which would, of course, be something of a trick since he wasn't supposed to be there at all, but over in Utah with papers to serve.

Still, it was something that needed to be done. "In the meantime, Boss, whyn't you give some thought to what we can do to figure out what Cotton and that crowd are up to with this charade of theirs."

"That I will, Longarm. That I will."

Longarm checked his watch. He'd told Deborah he would meet her back at the bench where she took her lunch once he was done talking with Billy. He was more anxious than ever now to find out what she'd learned about the possible survival of U.S. Attorney Terrell.

"You take care of yourself, Mr. Janus," Longarm said. "An' I'll be back to check up on your progress later."

"Do that, Doctor. You just do that," Billy said with a conspiratorial wink.

Chapter 36

"Pssst! Henry. Over here."

"Longarm. What are you doing here?"

"Waitin' for you, actually. I didn't want to miss you."

Henry glanced nervously down the street in both directions, but no one was paying the least bit of attention to them.

"It's all right, Henry. Do you have your keys with you?"

"Of course I do. Why do you ask."

"Because I got to get into the building, that's why."

"What building?"

"The Federal Building. What the hell else would I be needing your keys for?"

"You need to get into the office, Longarm?"

Longarm grinned at him. "Not ours. The U.S. attorney's."

"I don't understand."

"Then sit down here on the bench beside me an' I'll explain. First, though, do you happen to know if Cotton and his people have closed up an' gone for the evening?"

Henry snorted. "You won't find any of that crowd

159

working late. I'm sure they are gone." Henry seemed to think about that for a moment. Then his eyes got wider. "Longarm! Really. You don't intend . . ."

"Maybe you'd best not ask me that question, Henry. You might not wanta know the answer."

"Or perhaps I should."

"I saw Billy this afternoon, Henry. Here's what him and me got to thinking . . ."

Five minutes later Longarm was on his way the few short blocks to the Federal Building, Henry trudging grim-faced but determined at his side.

"I'm tellin' you, Henry, you don't have to get involved with this. I can handle it alone."

"You mean you can take all the heat yourself if you get caught," Henry retorted. "May I remind you that two pairs of eyes will get done with the job in half the time? If I am with you there is that much less chance of anyone being found out."

Longarm nodded. He should have known better than to think Henry would hand the job off to Longarm and walk away. The meek and bookish-appearing clerk had a core made of whang leather and spring steel. All the more so when the issue at hand involved his personal loyalty to Marshal Billy Vail. No, there was no way Henry would allow himself to be kept out of this even if Longarm wanted it. And the truth was that Henry was perfectly right in what he said. Two of them would have twice the chance of success that either one of them would have alone.

Henry used the keys on his ring to open the front door of the Federal Building. He carefully locked it behind them once they were inside.

The gas lamps in the corridors were turned to a low flame, and half of them were extinguished altogether. Longarm thought the dim, shadowy effect was more than a little bit spooky, but Henry did not so much as seem to notice. But then Henry spent a good many evenings alone in the office tending to the mountains of paperwork that kept the place running smoothly. Longarm tended to spend his evenings enjoying a drink, a meal, perhaps a little feminine companionship. He was not used to being in the building when it was empty like this.

Their footsteps rang hollowly on the flooring as they marched past the marshal's office and on down the hall to the somewhat larger and more nicely appointed suite of offices occupied by the U.S. attorney and his staff.

"I don't have a key to this door," Henry whispered.

"That's all right. I do."

Henry gave him a quizzical look, which Longarm ignored. Longarm took out his penknife and opened the short, stubby blade. He slipped the slim length of steel between the door and jamb, slid it up and down until he located the lock bar, and jimmied the lock sideways until he could insert the knife blade past the bar. A light tug on the handle and the door swung open.

"I don't think I could have gotten it open that quickly if I *did* have the key," Henry said.

"All it takes is a criminal touch," Longarm told him. "I think I woulda made one hell of a fine outlaw if I'd wanted to go into that line of work."

"You may be right." Henry started to push the door closed behind them.

"Leave it open," Longarm ordered.

"What if the night watchman comes by?"

Longarm grinned at him. "Hell, son, that's why I want you to leave it stand open. Whoever is on duty tonight is sure to know us. An' would we call attention to ourselves if we was up to something we oughtn't to be?"

"Oh. I see."

"Good. One more thing. If the watchman does come in to see what we're up to, don't tell him anything unless he asks. That's one of the first things that gives crooks away. They think they're suspected of something so they start telling lies to cover it over. If you just act like you got a right to be doing whatever it is you're doing, most often folks—even guards—will think you really do. So if Sam or Charlie or one of them comes in to see who's in the office late, just tell them hello an' let it go at that.''

"I wouldn't have thought of that," Henry said.

"Yeah, but you don't have the criminal frame of mind like I do.''

"I hope you don't expect me to regret the lack.''

Longarm smiled at him, then set about lighting every damn lamp in the place. Hey, they had nothing to hide there. No, sir, not a thing.

"Whyn't you take the files in the outer office here," Longarm suggested. "I'll look in Mr. Terrell's office. Or Cotton's, I s'pose it would be now.''

"I wonder whose it is at this point. You did say the U.S. attorney may still be alive, right?''

"That's right, I . . . oh, shit.''

"What's wrong, Longarm?''

Longarm rolled his eyes and shook his head. "That nurse friend of mine who was gonna find out if there is another hideout patient being kept under wraps.''

"Yes?''

"I was s'posed to take her out to dinner tonight. Right about now, as a matter of fact. She is gonna be pissed, I think." He shrugged. "Oh, well. Too late to worry about it now, so let's get busy an' see what Mr. Terrell's files can tell us.''

Chapter 37

"Are you sure this is the place, Longarm?"

"Pretty sure."

Henry glanced over his shoulder, then quickly in both directions down the street. "It doesn't look . . ."

"Safe?" Longarm suggested.

"That too."

"You don't find the sort of people we're looking for livin' real high on the hog."

"I suppose you are right. The only thing I hope is that we find them. Period," Henry said.

"We will if those reports are correct. Now . . . oops . . . act drunk," Longarm hissed in a low whisper.

Henry did not wait for an explanation. He hiccuped. Loudly. And swayed a little on his feet. Longarm put an arm around him as if helping to support Henry's weight, then started into the alley where they expected to find the cell of anarchists.

"You. Shtope," a thick, heavily accented voice said from the darkness.

"Shtope?" Longarm asked.

"Shto . . . shta . . . stope."

"Oh. Stop. You mean you want us to stop? What the hell for? Where's Bucktooth Annie? Ain't she working tonight?'' Longarm complained loudly. "Why ain't Annie here? Can't a fella even get laid around here without a bunch of strangers peeking over his shoulder?'' Longarm lurched closer to the man who, he could see now, was seated on a wooden crate smack in the middle of the narrow alley. There was no way to get deeper into the darkness without pushing past him.

"No hoor here, mister. Go 'way.''

"But my friend an' me, we're awful horny. We got money. You wanta see? We got lots o' money,'' Longarm said in a very slightly slurred voice as if he too had been tippling more than a man ought to, at least more than was sensible if he intended to stumble into dark alleys in the middle of the night.

The man leaned forward to see, whether with the intention of grabbing the money or simply from a natural impulse to look when one is told to, Longarm couldn't know.

What he did know was that the dumb sap had set himself up just right. A solid shot with Longarm's elbow—harder and less likely to suffer damage than the much more vulnerable knuckles—delivered to the point of the man's jaw sent his eyes rolling up in their sockets and knocked him cold.

"What was that for?'' Henry gasped.

"He's their lookout,'' Longarm explained.

"How did you know he was here? I couldn't see anything back here.''

"Hell, I couldn't either,'' Longarm admitted. "That's what ears are for. Mighty useful in the dark. I heard him moving around.''

Henry stepped over the guard and paused. "Now where?''

"There's light showing behind that cellar door down there. That must be the place.''

"And if it isn't?''

"Then don't shoot nobody. We can always apologize later."

Henry frowned and dragged a revolver from his pocket. Henry did not normally carry a weapon. It was not that he couldn't use one. He could, and could use it well when he had to, but it was not his habit. They'd had to stop in Billy Vail's office after they left the U.S. attorney's offices so Henry could open the marshal's safe and arm himself. Longarm drew his own ever-present Colt and edged forward. He wanted to get inside the cellar hideaway before that guard woke up and shouted an alarm.

"Ready?" he asked over his shoulder.

"I hope you are right about this," Henry said.

"That's two of us. All right now. Stay with me." Longarm inched down the stone steps and listened outside the closed door for a moment. He could hear voices inside, but could not make out what was being said.

Longarm raised his leg high, boot heel first, and kicked the door just above the lock.

Wood splintered and gave way, and the door slammed open, flooding the steps and alley with yellow lamplight.

Longarm bounded inside, Colt held at the ready.

The sight that greeted him there was enough to make a man's blood run cold.

Chapter 38

Why, these good folks—there seemed to be four of them at least, three men and a very pretty young woman—had themselves a dandy little factory set up in this run-down cellar beneath a crumbling tenement.

Not that there was anything wrong with that in itself. Longarm appreciated enterprise as much as the next fellow. The problem was with the product, not the effort.

These assholes were making bombs.

Lots of bombs.

One sweeping glance around the place showed two kegs of blasting powder and a box of high-grade dynamite. A workbench was hard against one wall. Its surface was covered with bits of this and that, which appeared to be bombs either already built or in the process of being built.

Some of them looked ordinary and innocent. Until Longarm noticed fuse cord poking out of them. There were glass bottles that had been converted into bombs. Plain old red bricks that had been hollowed out and stuffed with gunpowder, again with detonating caps and fuses attached, even two china dolls with bright blue eyes and golden yellow yarn for hair . . . and their bellies apparently full of death and destruction.

Longarm felt more than half sick when he took it all in. These sons of bitches were planning some serious mayhem, and God knows how many people—perhaps even small children judging from those dolls—were the potential targets of these animals.

"United States deputy marshals!" Longarm announced. "Move, damn you, an' you're dead!"

All four obligingly threw their hands up and stopped where they were, which was immediately in front of the workbench.

Behind them, closer to the door where Longarm and Henry now were, he could see several wooden crates partially filled with completed bombs.

All told, he guessed, there must have been forty, fifty bombs either already built or in various stages of assembly. Whatever these people planned, they were damned ambitious about it.

It was the woman who recovered her wits and spoke first. By that time Longarm already noted that Carl Beamon had been right; she was mighty nice-looking, if a bit on the skinny side. She was extraordinarily pale, like she rarely allowed sunlight to reach her, and had huge, liquid eyes. Her hair was black and long and glossy, although this woman—Longarm guessed she had barely reached her twenties—in no other way could ever remind him of Spotted Fawn or any other Indian maiden. The Indian women Longarm had known in the past were earthy, laughing creatures, filled with a zest for life and living that Longarm admired and appreciated.

This one—there was something about her. Something that made him think of vipers and scorpions. Something deadly and evil. He doubted she knew how to laugh or how to enjoy life. Take it perhaps, but not appreciate or enjoy it.

She turned and said something to her companions in a language Longarm neither knew nor recognized.

"I said don't move," Longarm told them firmly.

"Don't say nothing either. You're all under arrest on a charge of murder and—"

"You have no authority to arrest us," the young woman said in a cool, perfectly controlled voice.

"I'm a United States deputy marshal and—"

"We do not recognize the United States or any other government," she said.

"That's okay. You don't have to, honey. I reckon it'll be enough that the government recognizes you."

"Do not call me by any of your disgusting pet names. May we put our hands down now? It is tiring to stand so long like this." She continued to look at Longarm, but said something more in her own language, and the men began to fidget and shift from foot to foot.

"Stay just like you are, each of you," Longarm told them.

The woman barked out a sharp command, but none of the men moved. She repeated it, whatever it was, and looked plenty annoyed that they weren't doing whatever it was she told them.

"Longarm, I think we better put these people in manacles, then call for the local police to take them off our hands. We need to inventory everything here and start the paperwork on them," Henry told him.

"Yeah, I s'pose. Look, Henry, you go back out in the alley. Put some cuffs on that guy up there to make sure he don't cause any trouble, then go see if you can scare up some Denver cops to help us clean this mess up."

"Are you sure you won't need me?"

"None of us here is goin' anyplace until you get back," Longarm told him.

"I won't be long."

Longarm heard Henry take the steps two at a time behind him. Then he used his left hand to reach into his pocket for a cheroot. The Colt revolver in his right hand did not waver. "I want the four of you to move just a couple feet to my right. Over there by that wall, please."

He gestured with the barrel of the .44 to enforce the suggestion. "But slow, please. Everybody go nice an' slow an' nobody will have to get hurt."

The man on the right moved obediently in the direction Longarm wanted.

"That's fine. Now you." Longarm motioned with his revolver again and the second man, a young fella with greasy hair and a scrawny, wispy little excuse for a mustache, began sidling away from the workbench too.

"You're next, lady. Slow an' easy if you please."

The woman said something and seemed to stumble, then in a blur of motion grabbed at one of the lamps hung on the wall beside the work bench.

"Oh, shit," Longarm had time to mutter.

The woman had the lamp in one hand and a brick in the other, except the brick was no innocent chunk of fired red clay, but a completed bomb. Longarm could see the fuse cord dangling limp out of one end of it.

And he could imagine the sort of damage a bomb like that would do when it went off. Not only would there be the force of the explosion to contend with, there would also be a virtual storm of shards of brick flying in all directions, as deadly effective as the splinters of steel shrapnel from an artillery shell. Anyone within probably ten yards or so was sure to be injured at the very least, and anyone close to the blast would surely be killed.

"I don't know what you think you're gonna accomplish with that thing, lady, but let me tell you something. If you think you can bluff me . . ."

"Bluff, lawman? I do not bluff, never," the woman hissed.

One of the men said something to her, and she gave him a short, sneering answer. The man went pale.

"She will kill us all," the third man, who was standing immediately beside her, yelped in a high-pitched, overly shrill voice. The man sounded scared half out of his britches. Not that Longarm could blame him. The woman was holding the brick so the end of the fuse hung mighty damn close to the flame of the lamp in her other hand. "Leave us, mister, please, or she will blow us all up."

"Now that's kinda funny when you think about it," Longarm said. "You got no proper hostages so you think you can get me to back off by taking yourselves hostage? Bullshit. If you assholes wanta blow yourselves up, be my guests. Light that fuse an' be damned for all I care." He jammed the end of his cheroot between his teeth and glared at them.

Then Longarm's eyes widened in complete and unfeigned surprise as the crazy female did just about the last thing in the world he ever would have expected.

The idiot *did* light the fuse.

And boldly, unflinchingly, held the bomb high so it could complete its destructive work with maximum efficiency.

Jesus, Longarm had time to think as he threw himself backward toward the doorway.

Chapter 39

Henry still looked sick. Not that Longarm could blame him. Who would have thought that much blood could come out of such few people? It was positively amazing.

And at that the damage hadn't been nearly as bad as it might have been. Luckily only a few of the bombs on the worktable had gone off along with the one the young woman had deliberately exploded. Had all the explosive material in that cellar gone up, it would have brought the tenement down and probably half the other buildings in the block too.

As it was, there was one hell of a mess for the Denver police to clean up. And plenty of explanations that would have to be made later. At a more convenient time.

"Are you all right, Henry? You look kinda pale."

Henry swallowed and shivered a little, but all he said was, "I'm fine."

"You look like shit."

"Thank you. May I say the same for you?" While Henry was pale and sickly-looking in the bright light of late morning, Longarm was still half covered with dust and grime thrown up in clouds by the explosion. He had not yet had time to change clothes or clean up. There had been a meeting to hold and briefings to be given.

But that was earlier. Now they were in a hansom cab on their way across town.

"You'd feel better if we stopped an' got you something to eat," Longarm said. "We got time if you want."

The suggestion turned Henry a rather interesting shade of yellowish green. Henry had long since lost last night's supper, and he had not been willing to replace it this morning with any breakfast, settling for a few sips of sweet tea while Longarm had filled up with a hearty breakfast earlier.

"No, thank you," the clerk said.

"You'd feel better."

"Longarm, you are well and truly pissing me off."

"Sorry." Longarm settled back on the worn upholstery of the public conveyance and smoked a cigar in silence the rest of the way.

The cab delivered them outside the hospital, and Henry paid the driver, then followed Longarm inside and up to the third floor.

There was a different guard sitting outside Billy's door. "Sorry. No admittance, gents. The man inside is in protective custody," the guard told them.

"Is that so?" Longarm asked with a smile. Then, not in any mood to suffer horseshit from the likes of this asshole, he inserted the muzzle of his Colt about a quarter inch into the guard's left nostril.

The man's eyes went wide, and Henry leaned down and relieved him of his revolver, then said, "We are United States deputy marshals here on official business. Who would you happen to be?"

"I, uh . . . I . . ."

"Speak up now. Don't be shy."

"I, um, I'm just doing what I was told. You know? Protective custody. Really."

"Under whose protection?" Longarm asked, withdrawing the .44, but not very far.

"West Colorado Stockmen's Association," the unhappy guard told them.

"You have special law-enforcement powers under state law, is that right?" Henry asked. If so it was news to Longarm, but then he didn't pay all that much attention to stuff that did not directly concern him.

"Uh, yeah, I guess so."

"Let me tell you something, friend," Henry said. "Your authority does not exceed ours. So stay well out of our way and maybe you will not have to go to jail."

"Jail? Me? Marshal, I ain't done nothing but what I was told. An' that's the natural truth."

"Yeah, I'm sure it is," Longarm said. He jammed his Colt back into its holster and turned away, Henry following close behind. The guard vacated his chair at the earliest possible instant, and went tearing off down the hospital corridor like his life depended on it.

Longarm and Henry entered Billy Vail's room without knocking. Henry, Longarm saw without comment, looked close to tears when he saw the boss alive and well and lying in the narrow hospital bed there.

"Should be pretty much over with by now," Longarm said, pulling his watch out and checking the time. "The rest of the boys should've had time by now to pretty much round all of them up. The ones we know about anyway. Likely there's more, but we'll find out about all that when we've had a chance to talk to the big boys."

Before Billy could answer there was a commotion at the door, and Acting U.S. Attorney Cotton came bustling in. "You two had better have a good explanation for this or you will find yourselves out of work, I can assure you. You are interfering with an ongoing investigation."

"Is that so?" Longarm asked.

"Yes, it most certainly is. I just hope you have not destroyed all our work thus far. Hasn't Marshal Vail told you? He is here on an entirely voluntary basis, at the specific request of the president of the United States. We have good reasons for all this, reasons which you are in no position to understand, yet the two of you come charging in here like a pair of bulls in the proverbial china shop. You threaten one of my special deputies with a gun. You expose your own employer to danger. I . . . I don't know what other harm you may have caused.''

Cotton marched into the center of the room with two handsomely dressed young men behind him. Two men, Longarm noticed, who pretty much fit the description that John Boatwright had given him for the two men who claimed to be newspaper reporters. Perhaps also the two men Carl Beamon was supposed to meet the night he was killed? Longarm wouldn't have been surprised if that were so also.

"I'm sure my people didn't mean to interfere with your investigations, J. B.,'' Billy said.

"Perhaps not, Marshal, but you never know what damage they may have caused. Why, those Indians have sympathizers everywhere. You don't know who you can trust.''

"The Indians that are responsible for the bombing that killed Mrs. Troutman?'' Longarm asked.

"That's right. The Ute tribe. We have definitive proof now that they were behind the attack. The problem is that we do not yet know which misguided whites may be supporting them.''

"Now ain't that interesting,'' Longarm drawled. "You have proof, eh?''

"That's right, we do, and—''

"Commissioner Troutman knows all about it?'' Longarm asked.

"Of course he does, and believe me, Marshal, the commissioner will be most upset when he learns that your people are not cooperating.''

"You've seen Commissioner Troutman, J. B.?" Billy asked.

"As recently as last night," Cotton declared. "We had dinner together and talked about the results our people are obtaining."

"Now that's extra fascinating," Longarm said, "because the way I understand it, Commissioner Troutman was killed in that bomb blast. Him an' his lady too."

"That is what we wanted the public to believe," Cotton said smoothly. "The marshal here is in on the real truth. Has been all along. Tell him, Vail. Tell your man what you know."

"What I know, J. B., is that I haven't seen either the commissioner or the United States attorney. I've only seen you and the senator and the congressman. And of course Longarm here."

Cotton sniffed. "Yes. Longarm. Did he tell you that he is supposed to be on assignment elsewhere? Did he mention that he is neglecting his official duties while he charges around interfering in plans decided upon by wiser minds than his?"

"He did mention that to me, J. B. As a matter of fact, he did."

"I think a reprimand is in order at the very least, Marshal. I intend to recommend that. In writing, if you wish."

"Recommend anything you damn please, J. B. Although I don't know your recommendation will carry much weight. Not coming from a jail cell."

"Jail cell? Whatever are you talking about, Vail?"

"You made a lot of mistakes, J. B. One of the lesser ones was allowing me to lie around here with nothing much to do but think. Once Longarm brought me information to work with, I began trying to deduce just why you and your friends in the cattle industry would do a stupid thing like pretend the commissioner was still alive and why you would keep me here in this hospital. Do you know what I came up with, J. B.?''

Hell, Longarm wanted to hear the answer to that one, whether Cotton did or not. He knew they would get it eventually from the people that Smiley and Dutch and the rest of the boys were busy putting in handcuffs this morning. But it wasn't anything Longarm had quite worked out himself yet. He thought he had a part of it. But not everything.

"I know, of course, that the bombing was not done by the Utes," Vail went on. "My people cleared that up this morning when they found the anarchists' headquarters, complete with a stockpile of explosives, bomb-making equipment, and what have you. Those anarchists now are all either dead or in the custody of the Denver police.''

Longarm thought J. B. Cotton looked a mite pale upon receiving that unwelcome news.

"The bombing was unrelated to the plot you and your cronies developed. That had to be a spur-of-the-moment thing, of course. You had no time to plan it in advance, and in truth, J. B., you didn't do a particularly good job with the little time you had available.

"The thing is, you and your friends wanted so badly to take control of those free grazing lands from the Utes that you were willing to lie, to deceive even the president of the United States, to achieve your ends.''

"That is preposterous. You cannot believe . . .''

"Oh, but I do believe it, J. B. And we will prove it. Commissioner Troutman was killed in that explosion. He did not survive, as you so often assured me since. I have reliable witnesses who will swear to the timing of his death. Yet you went to a great deal of trouble to convince me that he was still alive. I had to wonder why you would take that risk. Your reasons come down to something as common and as tawdry as simple greed. Your friends, and therefore you, expect to make a great deal of profit if they can steal grazing rights from the rightful owners, the Ute nation. But the commissioner, or any honest replacement who might be sent out here by the president, was certain to report back in the Utes' favor. You did not want that.

"So you—you personally and whoever else was in on this behind you—came up with this lame scheme. You could inform the president that his friend Troutman was still alive but operating in secret as a means to protect himself against further attempts on his life. By doing that you could send false reports to the president and assure that the Utes would be stripped of their grazing rights in favor of you and your cronies. You had to keep me in the dark so I would corroborate your claims. Besides, you are thieves, but not murderers. You did not want to kill any of us who did not die in the bomb blast. You only wanted to make use of us. As for what you would do once your purposes were achieved, I suppose your intention has been to fake the commissioner's death, probably placing the blame for that on the Utes also. It almost has to be something on that order since you cannot come up with a live commissioner, not when the man has been dead all this time. But as long as the president believed him to be alive, you could get away with falsifying reports critical of the Utes and supportive of the cattlemen."

"You cannot possibly believe that," Cotton said.

"I not only believe it, J. B., I am sure the interrogations that are under way this very moment in other parts of the city will confirm it. You see, my people were summoned back from their assignments—assignments you gave them to keep them out of the way—yesterday. They gathered this morning to receive new assignments, and by now most of your friends should already be in custody, J. B. As you are yourself now. It is my distinct pleasure, Mr. Cotton, to place you under arrest."

"On what charge?" Cotton demanded.

"Murder," Longarm put in before Billy could respond.

"Murder? Don't be absurd, Long. Even if the marshal were right, which I deny totally, he said himself that murder was not part of the plan."

"Maybe not, but it happened."

"The bombing was an act of murder, yes, but I had nothing to do with that. Nothing."

"Oh, I believe you about that," Longarm said agreeably. "The murder I was talking about was Carl Beamon."

Cotton seemed genuinely puzzled. "Who?"

"Oh, nobody important. Just a fella that worked for the carriage-hire company. He saw something, knew something, maybe guessed something. Those boys standing behind you killed him to make sure he couldn't tell it an' point any fingers where they didn't belong."

"No, I . . ."

"But they did, Cotton. Didn't they bother tellin' you what they done? They killed that fella Beamon. An' being part of your conspiracy, the fact that they killed him for you an' your pals, in the eyes of the law, Cotton, makes you as guilty of murder as they are." Longarm smiled. "Check it out with a lawyer if you happen to know a good one."

"No!" the acting U.S. attorney shouted. "They couldn't. They can't have." He spun to face the two. "You idiots. Don't you know any better than to—"

The bodyguards, or whoever the hell they were, apparently had no intention of standing there while their own boss gave them away.

The one nearer the door grabbed his gun. The other wrapped an arm around J. B. Cotton's neck and held the lawyer in front of him like a shield.

"Look, dammit, we aren't going to swing for the likes of him and his friends," the one holding Cotton said. "We're going to back out of here nice and slow. Nobody has to get hurt. All we want is gone. Okay?"

"Not okay at all," Longarm said.

"You move, mister, I'll shoot this man."

"All right, shoot him," Longarm agreed.

"I'm not bluffing. I will shoot him."

"Mister, I'm not bluffing either. Go right ahead an' do whatever you think is best."

The one who did not have a human shield apparently did not much care for the direction the conversation was taking. He already had his gun in hand, and he leveled it at Longarm. Or tried to.

Before he could cock the single-action Colt, Longarm's gun filled the hospital room with thunder and with the stink of burnt gunpowder. The bodyguard took a slug in the chest and reeled backward, turning and falling headlong into the doorway, where he lay unmoving.

Cotton tried to pull away from the second man. He twisted and dropped to his knees, giving Longarm a clear shot.

The second killer was no quicker nor better than his partner had been. He went down with three bullets in him as Longarm, Henry, and Billy Vail fired almost simultaneously, knocking him off his feet and onto his back with blood gushing from a set of wounds in his chest and belly.

J. B. Cotton looked at his bodyguard and began to vomit.

"I didn't know about the murder," Billy said.

"Hell, Boss, there's lots of details we got to work out yet. But I'm sure Mr. Cotton an' his friends will be willin' to cooperate once they see the choice is between that or the gallows."

"Yes, I wouldn't be surprised. But what about Jason Terrell? Did he really survive the bombing too or was that just more of their lies?"

"The U.S. attorney is fine, Billy. He's down on the first floor, kept there just like you been. A nurse friend tells me he's got a busted eardrum an' likely won't ever hear as good as he used to, but apart from that, he's just fine.''

''Thank goodness.''

''Ready to get back to work now, Billy?''

''Damn right I am. Just as soon as I personally put handcuffs on Mr. Cotton here.''

Watch for

LONGARM AND THE WICKED SCHOOLMARM

235th novel in the exciting LONGARM series
from Jove

Coming in July!